THE GIRL IN PLAIN SIGHT

THE GIRL IN PLAIN SIGHT

THE LAST VAMPIRE™ BOOK 4

JUDITH BERENS   MARTHA CARR   MICHAEL ANDERLE

This book is a work of fiction.

All of the characters, organizations, and events portrayed in this novel are either products of the author's imagination or are used fictitiously. Sometimes both.

LMBPN Publishing
PMB 196, 2540 South Maryland Pkwy
Las Vegas, NV 89109

First US edition, July 2019
Print ISBN: 978-1-64202-374-9

THE GIRL IN PLAIN SIGHT TEAM

Thanks to the JIT Team

Daniel Weigert
Misty Roa
Micky Cocker
Paul Westman
Dorothy Lloyd

If we've missed anyone, please let us know!

Editor
SkyHunter Editing Team

DEDICATIONS

From Martha

To everyone who still believes in magic
and all the possibilities that holds.
To all the readers who make this
entire ride so much fun.
And to my son, Louie and so many wonderful friends who
remind me all the time of what
really matters and how wonderful
life can be in any given moment.

From Michael

To Family, Friends and
Those Who Love
To Read.
May We All Enjoy Grace
To Live The Life We Are
Called.

CHAPTER ONE

It was Winter Break after her first semester, and Vickie soon realized that the early years of high school could be disappointingly boring.

After the first two days of doing nothing, she cornered Alexis, who was in her room, reading a comic book on her bed under the light of the Christmas lights hung overhead.

"Can we do something?"

Her sister looked up from her comic book. "What do you want to do?"

She raised her palms at her sides, confused by the question. "Anything. I've done things every day since I got here, and now there's nothing going on for the next two and a half weeks."

"You have practice with the cross country team, right?"

"Not until next week. Meanwhile, I'm really bored here."

Alexis smiled as she laid the comic book in her lap. "Just enjoy it. My dad says the older you get, the more stuff you have to do. When you have the chance to do nothing, you're supposed to take it and run. There will be more than enough to do in a few weeks so be bored while you can."

Not willing to accept that answer, Vickie knocked on Craig's bedroom door. He welcomed her in and spun in his chair. "What do you need, sweetheart?"

"I'm bored."

He scratched his head. "You know, Alexis used to say that all the time. Her mom would always say, 'You're not bored, you're boring.' Either that or she'd come to me and I'd give her chores to do around the house until she got the point." He gave her a self-satisfied smile. "If you haven't noticed, she doesn't complain about being bored anymore." He stood from his chair. "But, since you're still technically new here, I'm willing to cut you some slack. Is there something I can do to help you not be bored anymore—other than hand you a dust rag?"

Eventually, the two of them came to an agreement. She could spend her Winter Break at the local library if he gave her a ride there. It was less than ten minutes away, it was a safe place to go where she wouldn't get in much trouble, and there would be so many books that she couldn't possibly be bored for long.

Her arrival at the library every weekday was a relief. The automatic doors made the now familiar *whoosh* sound as Vickie walked inside. She sighed with pleasure when the heat immediately warmed face.

What should I start with today? Maybe dig into some world history? Or read a biography of a movie star? Those old-timey stories fascinate me.

At the front of the library, near the entrance, were the new release stacks. The librarians liked to keep these filled with the latest books to be added to the library's system. She searched through the Young Adult shelf and came across a book called, *Thrice Bitten.*

With a smirk on her face, she held the book in her hands and admired the cover. The white-haired teenage vampire girl bared her fangs and her hands glowed from some indeterminate superpower that vampires had in that fictional world. *Teen vampire books are so far off, it's hilarious. If I could ever bring myself to read one, I'd probably be very amused.*

She put it back and walked up to the wide, blue staircase to the upper level of the library. The lower level was reserved for new releases, audiobooks, and the Children's Section. As always, the latter overflowed with haggard mothers who allowed their little ones to roam free. Most kids went stir-crazy from not being able to run around the back yard in a Wisconsin winter as much as they obviously could in summer.

There's too much noise down there anyway. She walked past the shelves of comic books and graphic novels. *I've seen Alexis read some of these. Sometime, I should dive in.*

Her stomach twisted. She stopped walking and grasped the comic book shelf to steady herself. With her eyes closed, she took several long, deep breaths.

You have control over this. Stay calm. You don't have to react. Breathe through it. It's only your body telling you that they're coming. It doesn't mean anything else.

They were the Circle, who had arrived in the country a couple of months ago. Vickie knew they were aware of her. Her senses had told her as much.

But she didn't know how close they were.

Once she'd managed to calm, she walked through the nonfiction section and settled on a book about the political unrest in the United States in the 1960s. She shuffled to a window seat at a small table where the sunshine reflected off the snow on the ground illuminated the pages so brightly, she almost had to squint.

She leafed through it and tried to pace herself. *Don't read too fast or you'll run out of books here in four days.*

Vickie caught movement out of the corner of her eye.

Cautiously, she looked ahead. From the back corner of the library, she could look down an aisle lined with shelf after shelf of nonfiction books.

Nothing out of the ordinary caught her attention.

She squinted and continued to watch for movement. *Relax. It's your imagination. Your senses are a little heightened so you think anyone walking past will be, like, something threatening. Go back to your book.*

Her mental admonition seemed to help, and she continued to read. A few pages later, she looked up again.

Between every third row was a large round pillar. The fourth one down caught her attention and she narrowed her eyes to focus on something dark at the foot of the column. *Is that a boot? A shoe? Did someone set a bag down there?*

Her stomach twisted tighter. She stood, hurried to the pillar, and peeked around it to see what—or who—it was.

Once again, she found absolutely nothing.

Jannik—one of the Circle members who had come to America— held his breath and crouched behind the nearby comic book section so as to not be seen. *Don't be caught. Your job is only to keep tabs on her today.*

He was tasked with watching Vickie. For months, that was all they did. They knew who she was and where she lived, went to school, and spent most of her time, but they hadn't attacked yet.

He risked a glance over the tops of the books on the open shelves as the vampire returned to the table.

A furtive glance confirmed that no one else had seen him either. He exhaled quietly and tried to control his nervous heart rate. He rose to his feet and looked around the pillar once more.

Gabriel would not disclose all the plans they had, but he was insistent that they watch her every day. Because the girl didn't appear to pose any immediate threat, the leader wanted to take his time, but it didn't make sense to the rest of the group.

Vickie turned to sit in her chair. This time, she saw the man's face peering at her from behind the pillar. She gritted her teeth. *I don't know who that is, but he's up to no good.*

She glanced around to make sure no one else was in that corner of the library. Jannik guessed what she planned to do and rushed hurriedly around to the comic book racks again.

He'd barely darted behind them when she tapped into her super-speed and hurtled toward the pillar. Blinded by her heightened emotional state, she overshot it and ran into one of the comic book shelves.

It tipped violently and books and pages scattered everywhere. The librarian at the desk near the top of the stairs bolted out of her chair. Jannik, who still crouched behind another shelf, leapt to his feet and ran in the other direction, although he tried to look as natural as possible.

Vickie stared at the destruction she'd caused with a spooked look on her face. *How did I let that happen?*

The damage was extensive. The metal of the shelf had been dented and buckled. Some of the comic books were torn. Pages still drifted in the air as the old librarian power-walked to the wreckage.

"What happened?" she shouted, the whisper rule clearly forgotten as she held her hands to her head in disbelief.

"I… I'm sorry…" The girl's face was frozen in shock.

The woman stepped around the carnage to gawk at her. "Did you do this?"

"It was an accident."

The librarian covered her mouth, her expression horrified. "It looks like someone ran into this with a car." She turned to Vickie. "Are you okay, sweetheart?"

At the bottom of the stairs, Jannik pulled his phone out and headed to the exit. "Gabriel, she nearly caught me this time. We have to take care of this before one of us is hurt." Unfortunately, their leader didn't agree.

The next week, Vickie joined a small handful of her cross country teammates and Coach Lueck at the Pettit National Ice Center down the road from the high school.

She climbed out of the car and waved to Craig as he drove off. The speed skater statue in front of the entrance towered over her. *I wonder why we practice here. This isn't a running arena. It's a skating arena.*

When she walked into the lobby, the coach greeted her with a smile. "Welcome to your first Pettit workout, Vickie. You'll love it. Or hate it. We'll see." He laughed as the two of them stepped through the large metal doors and into the rink area.

The other girls and the boys greeted her warmly when she walked in. They leaned against the bleachers as they waited to hear from Coach.

Lueck stepped in front of them and smiled. "It's our first winter workout, everyone. I'm glad to see so many of you here. As you know, track will come in spring, and I appreciate that you want to put in the extra time to improve yourselves in the off-season. This is the kind of work you do when you want to be winners, so I'm thrilled to see the dedication. The track surrounding the rink here is about a quarter-mile. It's not standard size, but it works well enough for our purposes. Go ahead and get ready, and I'll meet you over there at the starting line."

He jogged off and the team stripped off their outer layers of clothing. Some shivered immediately when the cold from the rink area reached their exposed skin.

Vickie looked out over the ice. A few families skated around with their children. Other individual speed skaters worked out and swung their arms as they careened across the ice. "Will these people watch us while we run around the rink?"

Krista laughed. "Kinda, yeah. But no one really watches us. They know there's a track here, so it's not uncommon for anyone to run on it. It's when we puke that we catch people's attention."

As they jogged to the starting line, she felt her stomach

twist again. She immediately scanned the area between the ice and the bleachers but saw no one.

Instead, she accidentally ran into Coach Lueck at the starting line and almost toppled him. He laughed it off. "Whoa, Vickie. You're a little too anxious to start running. You have to wait for me to yell go."

As she apologized, the doors on the far end of the ice swung open slowly. Jannik and Gabriel stepped through and moved quickly under the bleachers.

"I don't understand, sir," he pleaded with the leader. "Shouldn't we simply kill her already? Why do we have to watch her constantly?"

The leader shook his head. "This is the first vampire to exist in this world in centuries. There has to be a reason for her to be here. What if she is working to assemble a new race of these forsaken creatures? Killing her is foolish if she will lead us to others. The Circle has always been patient. We will wait for our moment to strike."

Throughout the workout, Vickie could feel the presence of the Circle. She stopped paying attention to her splits. Her mind raced faster than her legs did.

Where are they? Could they be hiding here? Are they on the ice? I don't see them on the bleachers. What do they want with me?

"Vickie!" Coach Lueck called out from the other side of the track. "Pace yourself."

She turned her head to see she was nearly half the track's length ahead of her teammates, who huffed and puffed through their workout while she ran effortlessly ahead of them.

Whoops. Pretend like you're tired.

CHAPTER TWO

Alexis pushed into the house and shivered as she shook the snow from her shoulders. "Brrrr. Boy, this snow won't stop today." She slipped her boots off on the rug at the door and stepped into the kitchen. "Mail's here. Vickie—schedules!"

The vampire came out of her room to join her at the kitchen table. The school schedules were mailed out the week before Winter Break ended. This was when they learned what lunch they had, when their study halls were, and what teachers they had for their classes.

Even though Alexis wanted to think of anything but school for a few more days, checking the new schedule was always an exciting activity.

Both girls tore the envelopes open and began to read through the details.

"Sweet!" Alexis pumped her fist. "I have Mrs. Braun, Mr. Schroeder, and Mr. Pluger this semester. I hit the jackpot on teachers."

Vickie congratulated her but her expression sank.

"We're still on different lunches. And no study hall together now, either."

"Darn." Her sister shook her head. "Well, I guess it's time to start making some friends."

She continued to study her schedule. "Who's Mr. Numerich? I don't think I've seen that teacher yet."

"Ugh." Alexis grabbed her schedule. "You signed up for general business class? Why?"

The vampire shrugged. "Why not? Is it that bad?"

"I've only heard bad things about Mr. Numerich."

When the first day of the new semester arrived that following Monday, Vickie held her breath as she walked into Mr. Numerich's classroom.

The atmosphere was a very specific kind of dreary. Few classrooms at Clear Lake High School were exciting in atmosphere—the science classrooms possibly the only exceptions—but Mr. Numerich's room was at a level all its own.

I didn't even know there was a classroom in here. She shook her head in surprise. It was at the very beginning of the English Hall, but the door was inset from the corridor so it didn't open into it directly. It was adjacent to a closet door, and most students assumed it was simply another closet.

The walls are green? Really? What a hideous color. And no windows. It's stuffy and lifeless in here. I'd better take a seat at the back.

She walked to the back row and sat. The room was far enough away from the hall that eventually, it felt like it was in a different building. *It's so quiet in here. And the lights are so dim. Was this previously a closet and they turned it into a classroom because they ran out of space or something?*

Seated at the front of the room behind his desk was a stocky man with large, thick glasses. His hair was a mixture of brown and gray, slightly feathered, and brushed back away from his forehead.

He wore a short-sleeved mustard-colored shirt that stretched over his ample gut and a long brown tie. The tip barely kissed his belt buckle and matched his brown pants.

Once the bell rang, he stood from his desk and looked at his new class of students with no expression on his face. He paced the front and waited for them to quiet before he launched into his introduction.

"Ladies and gentlemen, welcome to general business. My name is Mr. Numerich, and I am your instructor for this course." He punched the end of every sentence he spoke with an authoritative tone. "Before I pass out the syllabus, I would like to go over a few of the ground rules that you must know if you are to achieve success in this class, okay?"

As he spoke, Vickie was distracted by his physical tics. Between every other sentence, he craned his neck briefly, as if to stretch it. Every blink seemed deliberate and forceful. And before he stretched his neck, he would press his lips together. *Why does he keep doing that? It's all I can see now.*

"Rule Number One. There will be no talking out of turn in this class. Whenever you speak without having raised your hand first, there will be consequences. If you want your voice to be heard, raise your hand and wait to be called on. Many students in the past have raised their hand and begun speaking while their hand is still in the air. Do not do this."

That is a lot of words to use to tell us to be quiet.

He continued to pace and made deliberate eye contact with every student in the classroom. "Rule Number Two. If you submit an assignment late without a pre-approved excuse, you will receive an automatic zero."

"Whoa!" one boy in the front row protested when he heard this. "Are you serious?"

Mr. Numerich glared at him. "This will be your only warning to raise your hand before speaking."

The boy, Mike Arroyo, bristled at the warning. Vickie laughed, having had Mike in several other classes. *If that's the only warning he'll get all semester, it'll be a long one for him. That boy never shuts up.*

Mr. Numerich continued. "Yes, if your assignment or project is submitted late, it receives a zero."

Mike begrudgingly raised his hand before being called on. "That…uh… That seems extreme. Why does it have to be so strict?"

The teacher craned his neck and wore a knowing smirk as if he knew that particular question would arise. "We live in a world of consequences. This class is to teach you about how the real world works. There are times when being late with a payment or some paperwork results in devastating consequences for you. I intend to conduct this class like the real world and not shield you from it, so that you may learn from those mistakes."

The student raised his hand again. He obviously still tried to grasp this idea. "Can you give us an example?"

"Of course." He put his hands in his pockets and bounced on his heels. "Let's say you have a credit card. I don't recommend you get one, but this is a good example. In fact, this is a good example of why you shouldn't get one. You have a credit card with a balance of one thousand dollars on it. You signed up for this credit card because you received an offer in the mail for a new credit card with zero percent interest on the balance for twelve months. You have carried that balance since you signed up for it eight months ago, but you have kept up with the payments. Now, let's say you miss the payment by one day—twenty-four hours. Do you know what happens?"

The class responded with blank stares.

"Okay. If you miss that payment by one day, you will lose that zero percent interest rate. Now, the zero percent interest turns into thirty-three percent—that is Annual Percentage Rate. What has happened to your balance?" Once again, expressionless faces from the entire class were the only answer he received. "It is now over one thousand dollars. You lost one hundred dollars by being one day late on your payment. Of course, I am oversimplifying these numbers, but this is the consequence of being late. And in the grand scheme of things, it is a rather minor consequence. There are much bigger ones at stake, which we will learn about in this class."

Vickie squinted as she watched Mr. Numerich talk to the class. *He seems seriously hard-nosed. Almost too strict, actually. But I sense that he means well. He doesn't act this way to be mean. But man, can I deal with this guy for a whole semester?*

"And finally…" He stood resolutely at the front of the classroom. "There will be no masticating of the forbidden substance in my class." He cocked an eyebrow and waited for reactions.

Some of the kids whispered, "What?" The boys—including Mike Arroyo—stifled snickers at the word masticating.

April Keihl, sitting two seats in front of Vickie, raised her hand. "Um, what?"

Mr. Numerich nodded as he repeated himself. "There is no masticating of the forbidden substance in my class."

"What is the forbidden substance?"

He put his hands behind his back and puffed his chest out. "Chewing gum."

No gum? That's how he says no gum-chewing?

Mike Arroyo raised his hand once again. "You don't let anyone chew gum in this class?"

"That is correct."

"Why not?"

"I find it obnoxious. When you do so, you make it difficult for people to understand what you say, and you fill the air with the chewing and popping noises associated with the activity. I am not interested in dealing with that, so there is no masticating in this class."

Mike failed to hide his laughter. "Do you have to call it that?"

"That is a perfectly acceptable word for it."

Vickie leaned back and folded her arms. *He knows he's making them laugh. He knows that wording it this way makes all these people—especially the guys—giggle. What is it with this guy? Is he a goofball or is he a tyrant?*

Mr. Numerich passed out sheets of paper with the syllabus on them. She jotted a few notes on it and sighed quietly as she rested the side of her head on her fist. *Do I really want to be in this class? The atmosphere is terrible, the rules are super strict—maybe I could cancel this class. Or switch to another one? There has to be another option.*

What bothered her the most was the air in the room. *It's so stuffy in here. It's thick, and since no one can talk, it's silent and overbearing. Honestly, it makes me want to fall asleep. I don't know if I can breathe this air for a semester. It reminds me too much of the room I was hidden in for four hundred years. That's not really what I want to think about every time I'm in class, is it?*

CHAPTER THREE

The girls sat on the couch, watching an old episode of *Friends* on the TV.

"That apartment looks bigger than this house." Vickie pointed at the screen. "This is in…New York, right?" Alexis nodded. "Are apartments all that big in New York?"

The other girl drew her knees up to her chest and hugged her legs. "I don't think so. I'm sure most of them are *really* small. I've seen memes online about how unrealistic it is that they could afford those apartments. Like, it would cost five thousand dollars a month or something."

"Is that a lot?"

"Uh, yeah. You could rent, like, three entire houses in Milwaukee for that kind of money."

She tilted her head in thought. "Why would anyone live in New York, then? Shouldn't everyone live here if it costs less?"

"Don't ask me." Her sister rested her chin on her knees. "I'm not sure I understand why stuff costs so much in other parts of the country. I only know that it costs much more to live in New York, and they can charge that because people will pay it."

"It seems dumb."

Alexis smacked her lips. "And speaking of dumb, let's see how dinner is coming on. I'm starving." She dropped her feet to the floor and walked through the kitchen to the sliding glass door leading outside.

She pulled it open and winced when the snow pelted her in the face. "Dad! What's the ETA on dinner?"

Her father huddled under the hood of his coat and flames flared from the grill when he flipped the burgers. The constant sizzle as the snowflakes landed on the hot grate almost drowned her out. He closed the lid and waved his hand to get his daughter to back away from the door.

He stepped in and shivered as he slipped the untied boots from his feet. "Probably another fifteen minutes or so. The burgers are almost done, but I still have to get cheese on them. Can you do me a favor and have Vickie flip the fries?"

Alexis nodded and grabbed a potholder. "Vickie! Fries!" She pulled the oven door open and the piping-hot air surged into her the face. *I always forget about that. Ouch.* She wrapped the potholder around the edge of the pan and lifted the fries onto the stovetop.

Vickie walked into the room and grabbed the potholder. With a flick of her wrist, all the fries soared upward. She watched them fall one by one, moved the pan around, and caught each one until they all were scattered evenly on the pan.

The other girl giggled. "I never get tired of watching

that." She opened the oven and the vampire slid the pan in and reset the timer.

As her father rooted around in the drawers for the meat thermometer, she smiled and shook her head. "What is it about grilling in winter that you love so much?"

He chuckled with almost childlike cheerfulness. "Why not? We're Wisconsinites, girl. Everyone sits around all winter complaining about the weather. Then they get all hyped up when spring arrives and they can grill again. I say grill whenever you want to. The only thing better than a burger off the grill on the first day of spring is a one off the grill in January."

He found what he was searching for and gave his daughter a thumbs-up before he slipped his boots on again. "Leave 'em in for another ten minutes. That should do it. Thanks." With a deep breath, he pulled the glass door open and hurried out before he let too much snow in.

Alexis laughed quietly as she checked the timer, then walked to the patio door and looked through the glass. *Three inches of snow is falling and he is still committed to that grill. He picks the weirdest hills to die on.*

After the food was cooked, Vickie grabbed a round of Pepsis and they all sat at the table. "It smells good."

Craig folded his hands in front of him as the girls filled their plates. "Darn right it smells good. No one else on this block is grilling burgers at this time of year. Consider yourself lucky. You were found by the right family, Vickie."

Alexis shook her head. "Dad, there's probably a reason no one else is grilling this time of year."

"Yeah, they're weak." He stood to select a bun and

opened it on his plate. "So, the first week of school is over. How is everyone doing?"

"I'm doing fine." Alexis bit into her burger. *Man...I can't deny that the man knows how to make a good burger any time of the year. Mmmm.* "I have Mr. Festerling for biology class, so I was excited about that. He's cool. My other teachers are decent. I have a good round of them this semester."

Craig squirted a dollop of ketchup on his burger, put the bun on top of it, and poured more onto his plate for the fries. "What about you, Vickie? How are your teachers so far?"

"They're fine. Except for one I can't quite figure out."

"Numerich?" Alexis smirked.

"Yeah. Like, he has really strict rules, and the whole atmosphere in that classroom is almost suffocating."

He sat with his plate. "Does it bring back too many bad memories?"

"Actually, yes. It's not the same as actually being in a coffin for four hundred years, but it sure takes me back."

The other girl swirled one of her fries in ranch dressing, which made her father scowl from across the table. "You know, there are rumors about Mr. Numerich."

He arched an eyebrow. "What kind of rumors?"

She shrugged. "Nothing creepy. Apparently, he used to be a circus clown."

Vickie almost dropped her burger. "Oh, come on. Mr. Numerich? I can't imagine that guy doing anything fun."

Alexis took a bite of her burger and set it down on her plate. "I'm telling you, everyone talks about it. They say he was a circus clown for years until he gave it up to become a teacher."

"Why would someone quit being a clown to become a teacher?" The question puzzled her.

Craig glanced at her and shrugged. "Why would someone grow up to be a clown in the first place? They are creepy."

"Dad, you're literally sitting next to a vampire and talking about being scared of clowns. Really?"

He shrugged and waved his hand toward Vickie. "This, I can understand. It makes sense to me. Putting on makeup and baggy pants to make kids laugh? I don't know. It doesn't make sense when I say it out loud, but I know what I mean, and that's all that matters."

Both girls laughed at his assessment.

"Seriously, though, I don't know what to do. I can't imagine myself listening to this guy all semester."

Alexis shook her head. "You won't like all your teachers. Sometimes, you simply have to suck it up."

"I know. But between that classroom and his 'no masticating the forbidden substance' stuff, it's so stifling in there." She adopted a deep, mocking tone of voice as she impersonated Mr. Numerich. "It makes me anxious, and I don't think I'll learn anything."

Her sister twisted her face in confusion. "Did you say masticating? What does that mean?"

Vickie gave her an annoyed look. "It means chewing gum. He could say, 'No gum-chewing,' but he literally calls it 'masticating the forbidden substance.' That's the kinda stuff I'm talking about."

Craig swallowed another bite of food. "Why don't we sit down and discuss this after dinner? I want to take a look at the syllabus and see what this class is all about.

Besides, it's Alexis' turn to do the dishes." He shook his head as he looked at his plate. "That masticating thing is pretty funny, though."

"Joy." His daughter was great at sarcasm.

Once dinner was over, everyone piled their plates and silverware on the kitchen counter next to the sink. Craig patted Alexis on the shoulder as she stood in front of them and stared gloomily at the work ahead of her. "Look on the bright side. Since I grilled outside tonight, you don't have that many dishes to clean."

He retired to his chair in the living room, and Vickie brought in a sheet of paper. "This is the syllabus."

She handed it to him, and he leaned back in his chair and looked through it, reading out loud the lines that caught his attention. "Okay, let's see…future life skills, that's good…balance a budget…manage a checkbook… what to expect to pay in taxes… Can I take this class, too?"

The vampire laughed. "Put a wig on and you can go as me."

"Don't tempt me. Look, all this stuff is super-important in life. I think it's a great idea."

She sat in the other recliner and folded her arms. "I know the syllabus doesn't say it, but that atmosphere and that teacher make me so uncomfortable."

"Well, sure. Some classes do that. But you have to look at what you'll learn here. And this is solid stuff. I kinda wish I had a class like this when I was growing up. Besides, you don't want to push off your classes."

"What do you mean?"

"It's too late to switch classes. If you decide you don't want this one, you have to drop it entirely. They'll give you a zero, and you'll have to take an extra one later to catch up again."

Vickie raised her eyebrows. "That sounds like a lot of work."

"Yeah, it's almost like they don't want their students to do that." Craig smirked. "Not all classes are fun and interesting, but I bet if you give this one a chance, you'll find a way to make it worthwhile. There are good life skills in here. You might be surprised."

"I doubt it. But you're right, I should hang onto it. I don't want to take a zero."

He returned her syllabus to her. "Of course you don't. So hang in there. Worst-case scenario, it's done after a few months and you can move on from it. But I've always found that the teachers I hated the most were also the ones I admired the most. They work very hard for your respect."

CHAPTER FOUR

"Welcome back to another episode of *The Truth About... the Modern Family.* My name is Craig Watson, and I am a former-investigative-journalist-turned-stay-at-home-widower. On this show, I explore topics, issues, and concerns that today's families have to deal with. In today's episode, I would like to welcome Vickie back to the show."

"Hi, everyone." She had grown much more comfortable in front of the microphone over the past few weeks.

"You know, Vickie, we have many listeners who send us questions every week for us to answer on the show, and I wanted to do something of a light Q and A. I have a handful of the most popular questions here in front of me."

"Fire away. I love answering questions like these. Otherwise, I have to sit here and come up with interesting things to say on my own."

Craig laughed. "Our first question is from Bianca on Twitter. She asks, "Vickie, what made you decide to come with Craig and his daughter to America, specifically? How did the idea even come up in conversation, to begin with?' We've talked a fair amount on this show about your move here from Austria and we will some more in this episode. But would you like to share the story one more time for listeners who haven't caught up yet?"

Vickie straightened and scooted closer to the microphone. "Of course. So, Bianca, my parents were killed a while back. Um…I won't go into too much detail about how and why they were killed, but as you can imagine, it was an entirely unexpected death. I also had no living siblings either. I spent months before I met Craig and Alexis hanging around by myself and didn't do much of anything." *Boy, that was an understatement!* "I knew of distant relatives of mine who were in America, but I didn't have the money or resources to fly to them or contact them in any way."

"Right, when we met, there was already an understanding that we were related, but we didn't know how it mapped to a family tree or anything."

"Yes. And we still don't have all the facts. We work together on the ancestry lines so we can have a more complete history of our family and where we come from. I think that's always important—never forget where you come from."

"We know we're cousins." He laughed. "That much is certain. To what degree, I have no idea."

"Right. And that's okay because family is family. And anyway, when I mentioned that my family was no longer alive, I believe Alexis was the first one to bring up the idea."

"Yes. She said something along the lines of, 'Can we keep her?'"

"I heard that. She told me she felt that way when we all first met. We tried to work out a deal where I could come with you, and we took care of that part. It doesn't make for very interesting stories, though." She shrugged. "I was a little concerned about coming here, but I didn't feel I had too many options at home anymore."

"And why is that?"

"Because I am only fourteen years old. When you're fourteen, most of your self-worth comes from your parents. You don't have any professional connections. Everything revolves around your parents. If my main source of productivity and confidence was now dead, I needed to come up with a new plan."

"You had to learn to be independent."

"Exactly. But independence in a small European town isn't always so achievable. I'd become known as their kid instead of my own person."

"Everyone knew everyone?" She nodded in reply. "That's how a lot of America used to be. Small-town America still can operate that way. Milwaukee is weird in that it retains so much of its small-town identity but at the same time, is a big city in its own right."

"I think that's helped with the transition here. I can still have a little of that smaller feel to keep myself from being overwhelmed by it."

Craig wrote a few more notes and looked up. "You know, this might be a good time to talk about some of the things you had to adjust to when you moved here. How is life different in America than in Austria, and how has that affected your ability to assimilate here, both as a citizen and as a member of our family?"

Vickie glanced out the window at the freshly fallen snow that blanketed the yard while she thought for a moment. "You wear shoes in the house."

"What an odd place to start this conversation." He snorted. "You don't wear shoes in the house in Austria?"

She shook her head. "No. Most residential places and homes will have slippers at the front door. You change into them when you arrive at the house. You don't walk barefoot if you're a guest."

"It seems like a silly thing. Maybe it's a tradition that has long passed us by?"

Vickie raised a finger to stop him. "No, that's not it. It's about manners. You walk around outside and pick up who-knows-what on the bottoms of your shoes or boots. Then you trudge that around the house."

"You can't simply take your shoes off?"

"Not in someone else's home. That's considered unsanitary—not by everyone, of course, but definitely more than a few. What I find is that many traditions and unspoken rules in Europe are focused around respect for other people."

"How about some other differences?"

"Okay, let's see… I'll shoot them off rapid-fire. The drinking age is only sixteen there but twenty-one here. I ate more bread in Austria, but it seems to be some cardinal sin here—"

"That's for health reasons." Craig nodded. "An overabundance of carbs can really do damage to your system."

"Sure, but I ate fresh bread every day when I was home. Here? You need some kind of occasion to eat bread. As if I need a reason."

"Wisconsin's not too bad about bread, though." He winked at her. "We like our bread and our cheese here."

"And otherwise, you don't have any castles, there are massive stores here that sell everything under one roof, no street markets here in Milwaukee...the list goes on."

"Our next question is from Tim, and—oh, it's for me. 'Dear Craig, what's the hardest part about losing your wife and the hardest part of raising children as a single dad?' Thanks for the question, Tim."

"I'll have to let you handle this one." She laughed.

"Right. Well, Tim, to answer your first question, the hardest part of losing my wife has been the loneliness when I need her. I don't simply mean I get lonely when the house is empty. I do, but that's not the point. There are times as a parent, especially when parenting a teenager, that I wish I had my wife's guidance. She was an excellent mother, and she seemed to know what to do all the time. If I had a problem with Alexis or I struggled with my career —or anything that might need to be discussed with someone else—she was there for me. Not having that set of ears to listen to what I have to say has been very tough.

"And for the single dad question, for me, it's merely the fact that I am raising girls. I don't know much about them. At all. So being told that I had to raise one? And now two? Ugh. It's tough. Even dealing with dating in general at this age already makes me lose sleep at night."

"It's my turn to ask a question," Vickie said with a smile. "If you knew you'd have a hard time raising Alexis by yourself, why add another girl? Wouldn't it have been smarter to have only her for a while as you figured out all the details?"

"Yes, it totally would have. But I've learned over time that doing the right thing doesn't always seem smart at the time. Okay, I guess we've answered those two. But trust me, there are tons of others here so let's continue. 'Vickie, what's the most important way to get a family to blend together? How have you been able to successfully cross that gap and be in a peaceful, loving family with other people?'"

"I was fortunate enough that this family already had a gaping hole in it that needed to be filled. I don't believe for a second that I can actually fill a gap like that except perhaps in some ways. But they craved something, and I'm at least something. With this family, it really comes down to the daughter."

"Alexis adores you."

"Right. She and I are best friends. It's not really something you can force at all, but it remains the same. If you can get on the same page with the other people in the family and build rapport that way, you can strengthen that bond together and grow as a family."

"'Vickie, what is the biggest difference between your adopted family and your biological family?'"

Vickie laughed. *Can I say "vampires" and get away with it? Of course not.* "I don't think there's any value in focusing on the differences. Because they're already there, we can all see them and they don't need to be talked about. If there are some serious ones, we'll talk it out together, right? But we wouldn't harp on the differences. That's not productive. I'll tell you that I like the cooking better here than in my previous home."

Which isn't that hard to do, since you didn't really eat in that box. Craig smiled. "Vickie, I have one more for you, and it's from me. Since my daughter is a teenager and won't talk to me about her feelings often—although she likes me to think otherwise, but whatever—are there any struggles that you two are going through together?"

She closed her eyes for a moment and thought it over. "Yes. I think we both struggle for attention. In many ways, I don't want any attention—you know this. But I have also gone from being the only child that Mom and Dad worried about to a family where there is another child and the father works from home, and whatever. Alexis was an only child before I got here and had two parents."

"Now you vie for the attention of one parent you're trying to share?"

"Exactly. And I don't know how to fix that yet. But I have to wonder how many decisions she makes simply because she wants attention."

CHAPTER FIVE

The second week of the semester didn't start out any better than the first. Vickie sat in general business class, frustrated and bored, and tried to push away the stifling feeling of the atmosphere while being sure to follow all the strict rules that Mr. Numerich established.

But he was not the only teacher who had his own unique set of rules. Several had assigned seating. Others had their own way of grading papers and setting up homework assignments. And still others had zero tolerance policies for talking.

But every day, she sighed as she sat in the back row of the general business classroom. *The difference between all those other classes and this one is the atmosphere. It feels so suffocating in here. This is my only class without windows, it's my only class with green walls, and Mr. Numerich's speaking cadence might put me to sleep.*

"Today, we will talk about Alan Greenspan and the history of the Federal Reserve, okay?" Mr. Numerich would often stop and start sentences, all while craning his neck and pursing his lips.

This guy was a circus clown? I don't buy it. She would lean back and kill time imagining him in baggy pants, caked white makeup, a big red nose, and a wig that was bald on top with big red hair sticking out the sides, like Bozo The Clown. It would entertain her for a few minutes but then she would be brought back to reality, usually when Mike Arroyo spoke out of turn in front and ended up in trouble.

This class was not the only reason she had a hard time that semester. Without her breaks with Alexis during study hall every day, she felt rudderless. Her sister used to give her pep talks, walk her through certain situations, and give her a small midday breather from having to be normal.

Now that they didn't share a study hall period anymore, she was on her own.

She shuffled her feet as she walked into the school library and signed in. Mrs. Schumacher, the librarian, greeted her warmly as usual. Vickie smiled politely and walked around the large circular desk at the front of the library so that she could see what tables were open for studying.

On a good day, she could claim a table in the corner or any of the two-person tables lining the walls near the computer lab. That day, for whatever reason, they were full.

She turned to the more comfortable lounge chairs, but they were full as well.

Okay, if everyone is at a table, my only option is to sit with someone for a change. Find a bigger table that has a seat and sit, I guess. Now, who looks the least intimidating here?

The vampire had to move out of her comfort zone a little more, and she wasn't thrilled about it. But if she had to choose between talking to someone new or going back to regular study hall, she would suck it up and find a seat somewhere.

At first glance, no one looked promising. Abby, one of Megan Fitz's friends, sat at a four-person table, her books scattered all over the surface. *Hogging the whole thing for herself. Classic move from her. On one hand, I could sit with her and show her that I'm not really that bad a person. On the other hand, we would both be miserable and I might not accomplish anything. Pass.*

She gave up on that and scanned the room again. A large football player sat at another table and there was room for someone to join him. *He looks so intimidating, wearing his football jersey. Although it's nice to see a jock doing some studying. But how long did I take to talk to Eric? I don't have a crush on this guy but sitting with another boy would make me nervous. Pass.*

Finally, when she'd all but given up, her gaze settled on a girl who perched with one leg tucked under her butt, her chin supported by her fist while she jotted points in her notebook. Her hair was cropped below her ears, and she wore just enough makeup to look good, it seemed. *Another girl here to study, and she has room at her table. I don't know her, so it could go either way. Why not? It's worth trying.*

Vickie walked up to the table and leaned over. "Is anyone sitting here?" She smiled politely.

The girl looked up from her notes and gave her a warm smile that revealed her slightly crooked teeth. "Nope, have a seat."

A good sign. She already seems friendly. "I'm Vickie."

"Yeah, I know. I'm Tricia. Nice to meet you."

"Likewise. So, you know who I am already?"

Tricia nodded and set her pencil down. "Oh yeah. You're the girl who took it to Megan Fitz last semester. Everyone talked about it."

Uh oh. Bad sign. What do people think of me? I haven't thought about that before. "Well, um, yeah, Megan was being—"

The girl raised her hand to stop her from talking. "Megan sucks. She deserved it."

She exhaled sharply. *What a relief. I was worried I was the only one.* "Thanks. So you like working in the library too?"

"It beats study hall." Tricia shrugged. "At least here, I can get more comfortable and spread out a little. I spend all day sitting in those hard desks. It's nice to be able to mix it up."

"I totally get it. I'm the same way." *This girl and I seem to have things in common already. She prefers the library to study hall and hates Megan. It's not much, but it's a start.*

Her companion slipped a ponytail holder off her wrist and gathered her short dirty-blonde locks into a messy ponytail. "You're from Germany, right?"

"Um, Austria actually."

"Whatever. All the same." *No, it's not, but okay.* "When did you move here?"

"This summer."

"How can you speak the language, like, so great already? You seem fluent in English. I feel like I'm barely fluent in English and I've lived here for fifteen years." She laughed cheerfully.

"There are still things I need to learn. It's not that easy but I do my best. Of course, it helped that I had studied English for a long time." *Yeah, Vickie, what did it take you? Five minutes?*

"Well, that's cool. I wish I could learn something as well as you."

She's complimentary, makes decent conversation, and she likes the library. This isn't so bad. Tricia really seems nice. I haven't made any friends outside of Alexis' circle. Maybe Tricia could be a new friend of mine. We could hang out once in a while.

"So, you know Eric Wishman?"

Vickie's heart jumped for a second and she thought Tricia wanted to talk about her Eric. But Eric Wishman was a different classmate. "I know who he is, but I don't really know him."

"He's here sometimes—shaved head, plays football. Like, he's a really cool guy. I think he's hot. I keep hitting on him, but I don't know if he actually gets the point or not."

She's already confiding in me. "Why don't you ask him? See if he wants to go somewhere on a date or something. What's the worst that could happen? He says no?"

Tricia titled her head and curled her lip. "I don't know. He's so hot. I'm sure he has girls throwing themselves at him. I'm one of 'em so I should know." She laughed. "You'll see him in here sometime and you'll see what I mean. He has biceps for days. I don't know how he does it. But he's as dumb as a brick, too. A lot of those jocks are."

This was a little harsher than what Alexis had told her about athletes. Vickie remembered the conversation they'd had about it, and she had said, "Many of them coast on their ability to play sports. Some don't. Some work really hard to keep their grades up. It depends."

This girl openly branded all athletes as idiots. Before she could react to that, however, Tricia slid her open textbook across the table.

"Hey, what do you know about math?"

"Oh. I know enough. Do you need help?"

"Ugh, yeah. I can't figure this out."

"I took algebra last semester."

"Great. You're smart. Look this over and tell me what I'm doing wrong."

Vickie nodded and leaned over to see various diagrams of shapes with measurements noted alongside. "What math is this?"

"Math A. I'm a moron." She laughed sheepishly.

She nodded and tried not to react. *Math A is the remedial course. This is much further behind than the math I have taken.* "That doesn't mean you're a moron."

"Well, I suck at math, at least. Like, what are these letters? I don't understand that at all. I know math is numbers. Then they throw letters like these in and it screws me up completely."

The vampire shook her head as she started to explain the concept of x and y in math and how they were simply indicators that you had to calculate for those measurements. Tricia nodded slowly as she listened, although Vickie wasn't sure if any of it made sense to her.

CHAPTER SIX

Alexis sat on her bed and cradled the small mirror in her lap. She leaned back to check her eye makeup, blinked a couple of times, and moved her face closer to it again.

The lighting is a little weird in here tonight. She tilted the mirror and swiveled it on its hinge, then flipped the switch on her bedside lamp to add more light to the room. *That's a little better. Don't screw this up or you won't get many more of these chances.*

She put the eyeliner down and selected her lip liner. *Remember what Mom always said—not too much. Only enough to make yourself pop. With a little liner, you don't need lipstick.*

While she dragged the pencil across the outline of her lips, she heard a knock at the door.

"Yeah?"

The door swung open and Vickie walked in. She wore a forced smile on her face. "Hey. Are you excited about tonight?"

She smiled. "I am. But I'm also super-nervous."

"I don't blame you." The vampire sat on the edge of the bed. "I really didn't think your dad would agree to it."

"I think Dad is kinda reaching a point where he knows his little girl is growing up and he can't fight it." She closed the lip pencil, tossed it into her makeup bag, and leaned back on her hands. "I know the last year has been really hard, but time can't stop, either."

Vickie winked. "Sometimes it does."

"Right, but you know what I mean." Alexis giggled. "I've been reading this book…" She leaned over to pull a book with a bright pink cover off her nightstand. "It's called *Momless*. It's all about girls dealing with the loss of their mothers—whether that's by death or divorce or whatever. One thing they talk about is making sure you don't stop living your life because of it. Not having Mom here is really hard, but it's also important to remember that life has to go on."

The other girl nodded glumly. "That's what your mom would want, right?"

"Oh, my goodness, yes. She was not one to sit around and mope. If she knew I had grieved as much as I did—and I tried to keep it together as best I could—she would have been annoyed with me."

"She'd be really annoyed with your dad, then. He's still hurting more than a little."

"He is. And I know that's why he didn't want me to go on this date tonight. It's hard for him. He lost his wife and with me growing up, it's like he's losing his daughter a little too, even though he's not really."

"I think if he knows you're thinking about that, it won't hurt him nearly as much." Vickie folded her hands in her lap and looked away for a moment. *Of course, I don't want you to go on that date, either. But that's because you're going out with a Sang.* "Where did you two decide to go?"

"Ice skating. We'll actually go downtown to do it. There's a really cool park in the middle of the city. I've never been there before." She pushed off the bed and set her mirror and makeup bag on the top of her dresser. "I need to get a license soon, though, because having to meet dates with my dad driving is brutal."

Ice skating. Good. That's public. Unless Will wants to be outed, he won't try to do anything to her in public. I wonder if he's going with her willingly or if he's only doing it to be agreeable.

"What I really wonder is if any of the Christmas decorations will still be out." Alexis slipped a cardigan on over her cami and started buttoning it. "My mom and I used to go downtown every Christmas season to look at the setup. They have a park there next to the ice rink. Many of the inner-city kids get together and light it up. It's really cool."

"Why didn't we do that this year?"

"My dad doesn't like to go downtown. He's already kinda annoyed that we're going downtown today. Besides, that was something my mom and I did together by ourselves. It would feel kinda weird to go with my dad."

When she was ready to go, her father pulled the SUV out of the garage and Vickie wished her luck. While she watched the two of them drive off down the road, she bowed her head and wrestled with the anxiety that nagged at her.

Please don't let Will do anything to her. If he tries anything, make sure she can retaliate. Get her back here safely.

During the half-hour drive, few words were spoken. Alexis couldn't sit still, wondering how her first date alone with a boy would turn out—if it would be as magical and fun and romantic as it was in the movies.

Her father bit his nails compulsively as he sped down the freeway. *I'm not ready for this. I'm not ready for this. I'm not ready for this.* "You guys aren't going anywhere else, right?"

"No, Dad. We're staying at the ice rink until you come pick me up."

He continued to drive and took a few breaths as he squinted out the windshield at the setting sun. "Do you have your phone on you?"

"Where else would it be?"

"You keep that on, okay? I can see where you're at. If I see that you have your phone off, I'll blow my stack."

Alexis laughed. "Dad, relax. What are you worried about?"

He paused. "Nothing."

"I won't do anything you need to worry about. This is my first real date. I simply want to go out and have a good time. That's it. Ice skating and maybe some hot chocolate. We won't disappear or sneak off anywhere. I promise."

Craig looked at his daughter and saw sincerity in her eyes. She wore a mixture of desperation and sympathy on her face. "I'm sorry, honey. You know I trust you. I simply—"

"You don't trust other boys. I know."

They pulled up in front of Red Arrow Park in downtown Milwaukee. The shine of the streetlights made the fresh snow on the ground shimmer. Alexis pumped her fist.

"The Christmas lights are still on the big tree—look!" She pointed out the window at the massive tree towering next to the ice rink. They had draped it in blue Christmas lights for the season and hadn't removed them yet.

He smiled. *She still has that childlike innocence. She'll be fine.* "Do you see Will yet, or do you want me to wait?"

She almost pressed her nose up against the window when she tried to see out. Three picnic tables surrounded a local art sculpture at the entrance of the park. Will sat on top of one of these by himself with his hands in his pockets.

"There he is. Okay, love you, Dad."

"Have fun, sweetie." She leaned over and gave him a kiss on the cheek before she slid out of the car.

He watched her walk away from the vehicle toward a boy and inhaled deeply through his nostrils as a lump formed in his throat. *There she goes, old boy. On to another stage of her life. It's okay. She'll do great. You simply need to keep going.*

Will watched him drive away and turned his attention to his approaching girlfriend. "Hey."

"Hey." She walked up to him with a big smile on her face, closed her eyes, and leaned in for a kiss. He obliged and she took his hand as they walked to the Starbucks on the other side of the fence. "Have you ever been here before?"

"No."

"Okay, so we have to get skates first. They're in the coffee shop. Come on." She tugged at his arm while they walked in. Before long, they stood on the outside of the rink and watched the growing crowd of skaters circle the rink.

Carefully, they stepped out onto the ice themselves. Having rollerbladed a number of times, Alexis had a general feeling for how to skate. In minutes, she felt confident enough to let go of Will's hand and scoot on ahead of him.

It feels so weird to be out on my own like this, but I feel free. This is fun. But when she turned, she saw a usually expressionless Will stumbling awkwardly, his eyes wide and his mouth hanging open while he tried to stay upright.

She slowed and took his hand. "This way. Bend your knees a little. You need to throw your weight forward and push off."

For a few laps, he tried to keep up with her, but he didn't do a very good job of it. He consistently stumbled, tripped, and somehow managed to catch himself each time. While he never actually fell on the ice, none of the experience was enjoyable for him.

As they passed the entrance gate, he managed to shift to the side. "I'll sit out for a little while. Go ahead."

"Are you sure?"

"Yeah. It's fine. Go have fun."

Alexis turned away from him and skated on as he stepped off the ice and onto the rubber mats. Her mind raced with questions while she dodged around other skaters.

He's not having a good time, is he? Am I ruining this? Should I simply give up on skating and we can do something else? How could I screw up my first ever alone date like this?

When she made eye contact with him as she passed by, Will mustered a polite enough smile and waved at her, which reassured her enough to enjoy a few more laps.

Finally, she gave up. *He's simply sitting there. It's fine. Go do something else or he'll lose interest entirely.* She skated to the entrance and stepped off the ice. "Let's ditch these skates and get some hot chocolate."

"Are you sure? You can still go on if you want to."

She waved her hand. "Nah. It was fun, but I'm here to hang out with you, not with complete strangers on ice skates. Let's go."

They waddled across the sidewalk on their skates and back into Starbucks, where they exchanged them for their regular shoes and ordered a hot chocolate each.

"Sweet, there's a window table open. I'll stake our claim while you get the drinks." Alexis scurried off and ducked around other people to commandeer the table at the window. Soon, Will arrived with their hot chocolates and sat.

"What do you think of this place?" She looked out over the ice. "I know it's Starbucks, but it's a little different than the usual ones, right?"

He nodded as he looked around. "Yeah, it's fine. I'm not a big fan of the huge crowds."

"I know, but if you wanted to avoid the huge crowds, you should have come here on, like, a Monday night or something." She laughed.

Will didn't hear much of what she said, however. In order to wrap the headband around her head to keep her ears warm, Alexis had pulled her hair up into a ponytail and exposed her neck.

The temptation this presented was almost too much to bear. His insides burned as he glanced constantly at her and imagined himself sinking his fangs into her flesh and having a quick meal.

I haven't been nourished in months. The human food doesn't do the trick. I need to have her blood.

She was filled with a different kind of warm feeling. *Is he staring at me? He's staring at me. Oh, man, I was worried he didn't like me, but here he is, staring right at me. He thinks I'm cute.*

Once they had finished the hot chocolate, Alexis wanted to compromise and go for a walk together. They strolled hand-in-hand through Red Arrow Park, admired what was left of the Christmas lights, and watched the vapor of their breath float into the air. She couldn't help but feel satisfied. *Despite all the problems we had and all the hiccups, this actually feels right.*

CHAPTER SEVEN

Vickie stood in the kitchen and stared out at the field from the bay window. *She's a big girl. She'll be okay. They're out in public. She'll be okay. This is fine. She's fine. Don't preoccupy yourself with this.*

Craig walked in through the side door and stopped, his concern evident on his face. "Are you okay?"

She turned to face him. They both exchanged expressions of worry. Neither of them wanted Alexis out on that date. "I'm fine." She spoke with a very unconvincing tone. "How about you?"

His wasn't much better. "I'm fine too, I guess. I'm a father, so I worry about the girl, you know?"

The vampire nodded. "I'm more worried about the guy."

He chuckled. "Me too. I'll get dinner started. Maybe we can take our minds off everything."

Vickie walked across the kitchen and pulled a Pepsi out of the fridge. "What are we having tonight?"

He clapped his hands and rubbed them together in anticipation. "I'm frying shrimp."

She took a few steps back and laughed. "Why are you so excited about a meal?"

"Aw, you don't understand." *Calm down. Don't overcompensate for how you're feeling. Act normal.* "Fried shrimp—especially homemade—is one of my favorite meals. And it just so happens that Alexis doesn't like it. I hate making meals for one, usually, so I haven't made it for ages. With her gone tonight, I can let loose."

Vickie sat at the kitchen table and popped the top on her soda while Craig pulled a bag of shrimp out of the freezer and dumped its contents into a large stainless-steel mixing bowl. He placed the bowl in the sink and filled it with cold water. "How have you been feeling lately?"

She looked up from her can. "Good, I guess. Why?"

"No, I mean, the *feeling*. That thing that makes me have to do home repairs." He smirked and made sure she knew he was joking. "Have you felt like you're in danger lately? What's the scoop?"

"Oh, that." She took another swig of her soda. "It's weird. I feel like I'm starting to at least have a little control over it, so I'm not constantly worried about revealing myself to other people."

"That's a good thing. I know you struggle with that, and we definitely struggle with having to keep you from getting in trouble. That's a win-win for everyone. And it means you're not having such a hard time anymore?"

She inhaled through her clenched teeth. "I don't know. It's stronger at different times, but it's always there. I wonder if I'm simply getting used to constantly feeling like

I'm in danger. If I'm at school, the feeling is fairly weak. If I'm out at the Pettit Center for a workout? Then it's strong and very distracting. Here at home? Weak. In the car on the way to school? Very strong. I can't quite pinpoint what causes it, but there are definitely times where it feels much stronger and more frustrating than other times."

Craig placed a wok on the stovetop and retrieved a jug of peanut oil. "And you said this has to do with the Circle, right?"

The vampire nodded. "I believe so. I believe they are coming, if they're not here already. I know enough about these emotions to be able to discern that much."

"Well, I won't let anything happen to you." He twisted the cap of the jug off and poured a few inches of oil into the wok.

"How can you be so sure?"

He replaced and stowed the container in the cabinet. "I have an insurance policy for such a thing."

"An insurance policy? That pays for things, right? What does insurance have to do with what we're talking about? It can't keep you safe."

Craig laughed. "Not like that. It's more of a figure of speech. Hang on." He disappeared down the hallway, then returned with a long-barreled shotgun in his hand. With a broad smile on his face, he held the weapon up to reveal the sleek, matte-blue barrel and wood-finished handle. "This is what I meant. This is my insurance policy."

Vickie tilted her head and squinted as she studied it curiously. "Now I'm really confused."

He turned the burner on to start heating the oil. "When I say this is my insurance policy, I mean that I have this here in case I need to protect my family. This is insurance in case of attack. It's a Remington 870 Hardwood Home Defense Shotgun. I simply have to pump 'n shoot. It holds four to six rounds of ammo— enough to ward off any attackers to my home."

She was impressed. "I didn't know you had a gun. Does Alexis know?" He shook his head. "Why not?"

Craig placed it on the kitchen counter and dumped the water out of the bowl that had stood in the sink. "I know it looks like I'm bragging about this, but I'm not. I'm only showing it to you because I want you to know that you're protected in case of an emergency. Alexis doesn't know about it because I don't want to worry her, and I don't want to have people talking to me about whether or not I should have a gun."

"Do you think she would have a problem with it?"

He stared at it for a moment. "I don't know. She might, but she also might not. We've never talked about guns. But I don't keep it for fun. I keep it safely locked away for when an emergency comes up. That's it."

"Have you ever shot it?" Vickie took another sip of her Pepsi.

"Yeah, but only at the gun range. I've never shot anyone, only targets. I want to make sure I'm a responsible owner, so I got certified for it and I took lessons, and I practice occasionally down at the range."

"You didn't use it when we were being robbed." She thought back to when she had to disable the criminals who broke into their garage. "We were all in danger then, right? If you had a gun, why didn't you get it?"

He shrugged. "Because I had a Vickie here instead." He

chuckled. "Seriously, your powers are much stronger than this stupid gun. But I assume you have some issues with your powers."

She frowned at him. "Why do you say that?"

"Because you are talking about how worried you are of the Circle. That means you feel threatened. And you're stronger and faster than all of them. These guys are only humans who believe vampires should be dead. They can't be that big a threat, can they?"

The vampire rubbed her forehead. "Yeah, that's how I should feel."

"But you don't?" He proceeded to pull the shells off the shrimp. "What makes you think your powers won't hold up to the Circle if they really did show up here?"

"Think about it like this. My powers are not my own. They were passed down to me. You humans talk so much about the genetics behind hair color and eye color and the same is true of vampires. Our powers are inherited from our parents. My parents had the same powers I do."

Craig nodded slowly. "Oh, so you think that the Circle can kill you despite your powers?"

"I don't see why not." She squirmed in her chair. "My parents were cut down. Everyone I knew was murdered, actually. If they managed to kill some of the most powerful vampires in this world, it means they know something I don't. I have no idea what that is, but it terrifies me."

He pointed to the shotgun before he dumped breadcrumbs in a small bowl. "That's why we need her. She's our insurance policy. We don't use it unless we have to, okay? If your powers are tapped out and you can't do anything anymore, we need a backup plan."

Vickie shrugged. "I guess so. It makes sense. Guns were the one thing my family never owned."

"Well, it becomes more common the further along in history you get. I'm happy to have it if it gives me an option to make my family feel safe." He cracked an egg into another bowl and mixed it with a fork. "Switching gears to something more lighthearted, I have money for you."

Her ears perked up. "Seriously? Money? What for?"

"I received payouts from ads I've run on the podcast. You and Alexis are both guests on the show and the inspiration behind the show. I thought it was only fair that the two of you get a cut of it."

"How much?"

"Your cut is eight hundred dollars. Alexis gets five hundred dollars."

She squealed with delight. *That's a lot of money, I think. Yes! I can't wait to get it.* "Wait, why does Alexis get less money?"

"She's done less work. She hasn't been on the podcast as often as you have, and you turned our family into the modern family that we talk about on the show. You get a little extra."

The vampire shook her head in disbelief. "I can't believe I'll have money of my own. This is so cool. And only for sitting in a chair and talking for a little while. I used to have to work in the fields all the time to get even what would equal a few dollars."

Craig dunked the peeled shrimp into the egg mixture and into the breadcrumbs before he finally dropped them into the hot oil. It hissed and bubbled when the food submerged. "Yeah, things are going well with the podcast.

I'm thrilled so far. The bills are paid, and I can slice off a little for you both. Life is good."

Vickie leaned back in her chair. "Eight hundred dollars. That sounds like a lot of money. Is it a lot of money?"

He moved the shrimp around in the oil as it cooked. "It depends on your perspective. If I have eight hundred dollars and I have to sit down and pay bills, it's not a lot of money. But if you're a high school student with no financial responsibilities, that's a good chunk of change."

Before long, the two of them dined together at the kitchen table on fried shrimp with cocktail sauce and tater tots on the side. He enjoyed every minute of the meal.

It's nice to have one daughter here while the other one is out, anyway. She is starting to really feel like family.

"When do I get my money?"

He laughed. *A little too much like family.* "We'll open a bank account for you, and I can deposit your earnings in there. You'll have your own debit card and you can start learning how to manage your own money. That general business class might come in handy."

CHAPTER EIGHT

Some things, however small they might seem, were definitely worse than others. Vickie sighed as she pulled the paper bag from her locker and slammed it shut.

She used to look forward to lunch. Last semester, she was able to spend her entire lunch period with Eric. They'd flirt, talk about their lives—to a point—and get to know one another. She appreciated getting to know Eric on a personal level. It was their time, even with Jess there.

This semester, however, that would no longer be the case. Eric, Jess, and Alexis were all on the first lunch hour. Vickie was on the second with Jamie.

At first, she considered simply going to the library. It was considered a free hour, so why not? But it didn't last long. *If only food was allowed there. I couldn't believe how hungry I got. I guess that's why not too many students go to the library for lunch.*

The vampire entered the bustling cafeteria and dropped her bag at her regular table. Jamie was already there with her bagged lunch, and she smiled warmly when she saw her approach.

"Hey."

"Hey. I have to get a milk. I'll be right back." *Jamie is such a nice girl anyway. It's fine that you have to sit with her. You could do a lot worse.*

While she waited in line for milk, she saw Megan Fitz out of the corner of her eye. Normally, this would jog memories of being humiliated and frustrated. This time, however, she felt more confident. Megan had been cut down after losing her bet in physical science.

On the first day of the semester, Vickie had made the girl wear a long, flowery dress with a white cardigan over the top. It wasn't crazy, but it was very much out of style for the trend-following Megan. She was dressed like a frumpy old grandmother.

In addition to that, she applied liberal amounts of eye shadow and lipstick for her. She looked like an old grandma who had applied her own makeup at ninety years old.

Whenever I see Megan, I'll smile. I can always remember that outfit. It was a fun day.

Vickie paid for her milk and sat with Jamie to discuss the day so far. "How's dealing with Paul in your English lit class? I know you've been creeped out by him lately."

The other girl twisted her face in disgust. "Oh, you'll never believe what happened. Paul sits right next to me, okay? We went through class like usual, whatever, and I crossed my legs in front of me. While I do that, Paul looks down and sees my feet off to his side. Next thing I know, he touched my feet. Ugh!"

She took a bite of her sandwich and gave her companion a weird look. "What do you mean, he touched your feet?"

"Exactly how it sounds. I have a really weird thing about feet. I don't know why, but I do." She shivered in disgust. "Feet are disgusting. Don't touch them and don't look at them if you can avoid it. Just...no. No feet."

"But, like, how did he touch your feet? Just took his finger and touched them?"

Jamie's eyes grew even wider. "No, that's what's so gross about it. He actually ran his hand up my foot, like he was petting it or something."

Vickie nearly burst out laughing. *What a strange thing to be weird about—feet.* "They're only feet. Everyone has them. You walk on them. That's about it. What makes them gross?"

"They just are."

"You wouldn't get, like, a foot massage or something?"

"Oh! Gross. No way. No way."

While her foot freak-out amused the vampire, anyone would have been grossed out by Paul Engelhardt. He was one of the creepiest guys in their class. Short, skinny, and obnoxious, he always wore t-shirts emblazoned with the latest craze in professional wrestling. His greasy red hair was already thinning at fifteen years old, and he seemed to take great delight in making people feel uncomfortable.

"Let's change the subject." Jamie squirmed in her chair. "I need to occupy myself with something else or I'll think about this all day. Yuck."

Vickie pulled an apple out of her lunch bag and sunk

her teeth into it. "I didn't realize Megan Fitz was in this lunch hour."

"Ugh, is she?" The girl looked around the cafeteria. "Oh, sure enough, there she is. I bet she leaves you alone now that you gained the upper hand over her again. How many times does she need to punish herself by picking a fight with you?"

"I hope so." She sighed. "I'm tired of dealing with her. I don't even know why she picked on me in the first place. What is the point?"

Jamie raised a finger. "Megan is an insecure bully. She picks on people to get her own confidence up. That's all. She thought you were an easy target."

"Obviously, I'm not, though. I've fought back repeatedly. What could she possibly want to do to me if I've proven to her that I'm not a pushover?" She ran her fingers through her hair.

"It's not about that anymore with her, then. Now, it's about revenge."

"You make this sound ridiculous."

"It is ridiculous." Jamie laughed. "I don't know why she keeps doing it either. I think it's funny that she does because she ends up the one embarrassed at the end of it. You'd think she would learn by now."

"I'm running out of ways to teach her." She shook her head.

As the two girls chatted, Vickie reminded herself of how sweet Jamie really was. *Maybe this lunch hour will be a good one. It's nice to have one-on-one time with Jamie. She's great. I should take advantage of any chance I can get to build deeper friendships.*

Lunch was almost over, but she was still a little hungry. "Hang on. Let me use the vending machine. Maybe a Snickers bar will top me off."

She stood and walked to the far end of the cafeteria, where the door to a small room filled with various vending machines stood wide open. The humming noise when she walked into the room seemed almost deafening.

Let's see...which one has the Snickers? Here we go—

"You and Jamie sure seem to be pals these days."

Vickie spun and tried to keep the dismay out of her expression. Megan Fitz stood in the doorway with a smirk on her face.

"What do you want, Megan?"

"Hey, I'm only waiting for my turn at the vending machines."

Yeah, right. "Yes, Jamie and I are friends, Megan. What about it?"

The girl stepped into the room slowly and deliberately and shuffled her feet as if she wanted to maximize the annoyance factor. "I merely think that's funny."

"Why?" She sighed loudly, knowing the girl was setting her up for something. The problem was, she didn't know what.

"Like, given her history and stuff."

Vickie inserted a couple of dollar bills and pressed the buttons to release a Snickers bar. "What history? From everything I know about Jamie, she's a sweetheart."

Megan raised her eyebrows and looked at the floor. "Just saying...I thought you two wouldn't be very friendly at all."

"Megan, do you actually have something to say or will

you dance around it for a few more minutes? I would like to eat this before I have to go to class." She snatched her Snickers bar from the slot.

"Look, I only know there's a history between Eric and Jamie, that's all. And since you're dating Eric now, I thought that would create conflict." The girl stepped forward and inserted money into the vending machine, although she darted sly glances at her.

Vickie stepped aside, her gaze still on Megan. "What history?" *She's lying to you. Come on. Don't let her get inside your head. You know better than this.*

"Please...half the school knows Eric has had a thing for Jamie since we all started high school. She would make him feel like he had a chance and then pull the rug out from under him."

She shook her head. "That doesn't sound like Jamie."

"Girl, you're still new here. Don't act like you know everything yet. Those two have been close for two years, but Eric has always wanted her. You were simply the second choice." She grabbed a bag of chips out and walked to the door, then stopped to face her again. "I wouldn't be surprised if she finally gave him the time of day and he dropped you immediately so he could date her."

"That's ridiculous. Eric and I are doing just fine."

Megan shrugged. "Sure you are. You two are cute together. You're his second choice, though. He wouldn't leave you because he didn't like you, but I bet he would leave you quickly if Jamie came a-calling."

"You're lying. This is really desperate, Megan. You only want me to worry about him and stuff. This is dumb."

"Hmm. Maybe I am desperate. But I bet if you asked

anyone who knew Eric at all, they would tell you the same thing. He wants Jamie. And the only reason you're with him is because he couldn't have her." She pulled the bag of chips open, popped one in her mouth, and crunched it loudly as she walked away.

The vampire began walking back to the table. *That's stupid. Why would she say something so dumb? Eric likes me and I like him. Megan lies all the time and she has good reason to lie to me. Do not fall for this, Vickie. You're not second choice. You're a big part of Eric's life now. Be happy.*

But as she approached the table, where Jamie waited quietly, she started looking at her friend in a different light.

Jamie is cute. She's been friends with Eric for a long time. They do have a history. Alexis would know, wouldn't she? If half the school knows, she would have to know. But why wouldn't she tell me that if it's the truth? Either she doesn't know about it, or it's not that big a deal for her. Something doesn't add up here.

"Did you get your Snickers?" Jamie beamed.

"Yep." She waved it around. "I ran into Megan Fitz there."

"Oh, great. What did she say this time?"

Vickie shrugged. "Nothing, really. Only a pathetic little lie. She's trying to throw me off and I won't let her."

"Good for you. Don't give her the opportunity."

She really is such a sweet girl.

CHAPTER NINE

"Are you girls going to bed soon?" Craig stretched as he pushed out of his chair in the living room. Vickie watched TV, while Alexis sprawled on the couch and swiped around on her phone. "It's getting late."

"Soon, Dad. I'm getting tired too."

He wished them both goodnight as he disappeared down the hallway and retired to his bedroom. Once she heard the bedroom door shut, Vickie turned to Alexis. "I have a question for you."

"What's up?"

"This is probably stupid, I know. I talked to Megan Fitz the other day—"

"Hang on." Alexis raised her palm. "Why did you talk to Megan? Haven't you endured enough punishment? And for that matter, hasn't she?"

She shrugged. "We ran into each other in the cafeteria, that's all. I wasn't talking to her on purpose. And besides, she is the one who started the conversation."

"Of course she was. Continue."

"Anyway, she talked about me and Eric and she made a comment about Eric liking Jamie."

Alexis looked up from her phone. *Uh oh.* "What did she say?"

"She said that he has a thing for her and always has. That I was the second choice for his attention because he loves Jamie and wishes he could be with her."

Her sister rolled her eyes. "I wouldn't go that far."

"Hang on, so you know this? You know that Eric likes Jamie?"

"It's not that simple." She sat up and slipped her phone in her pocket. "Like...yes, Eric has had a crush on Jamie since forever. That much is true."

Vickie stood quickly. "And you never thought to tell me this?"

"No."

"Why not? That sounds like important information."

"Because Jamie doesn't like Eric that way. I'm close to both of them, so I know how this goes."

The blood rushed to her face. "And what if Jamie suddenly decides one day that she likes Eric? That's happened before."

"It won't happen here." Alexis gave her a confident nod.

"You don't know that. People fall for other people all the time."

"Right, but not like this. Look, part of the reason he liked her is because she is so innocent and sweet. She's super-friendly, and Eric, like a lot of guys, interprets that as being flirty. She's cute, so he sees a cute girl flirting with him and thinks he has a chance. He asks her out, she says no, and everyone moves on with their lives."

"I can't believe you didn't say anything." Vickie shook her head in disbelief.

"Okay, so you tell me what gets accomplished, Vickie. If I tell you, you get so jealous that you break up with him, make everything weird between you two, and everything gets weird between you and Jamie. Things are already kinda weird sometimes between Jamie and Eric. Then I might as well hang out with Jess the whole time because the rest of my friendships are ruined."

"So there's nothing to worry about?" She sat next to Alexis on the couch.

"Nothing. I would have told you if it would have made any difference. Seriously. There's nothing to worry about between them. And if you don't believe me, talk to Eric yourself. He's a good guy. He would tell you."

That night, Vickie crawled into bed and tried to fall asleep. *I hope I don't lie awake all night worrying about Eric and Jamie. That would be stupid.*

Fortunately, she fell asleep quickly but was roused awake a few hours later by a sharp twisting pain in her stomach. She grunted as she woke up.

What on Earth? What's happening? Why is my body warning me? Is someone close? Is the Circle getting close?

When the pain refused to subside, she rose to her feet and blinked a few times. In the darkness, an orange glow shined from behind her shade. She peered around it and her stomach twisted even more. *Who is that?*

A man stood outside her bedroom window and clutched a flaming torch that he raised ominously. He was motionless, and she couldn't see any distinguishing features about him because his face was covered by the hood of the long, black robe he wore.

She stumbled back, then quietly opened the door to her bedroom. *Let them sleep. This is my fight.* Cautiously, she looked out the patio door and froze. Another mystery man stood there in the same kind of robe with a torch and yet another out on the driveway. *They have me surrounded. I can't go anywhere else without going right past them. What am I supposed to do?* She stood in the hallway and breathed slowly and deliberately to remain calm.

The vigilantes outside were excited to do what they had set out to do. In the driveway, Gabriel held both a torch and the sword in his hands. *She has to come out this way. And when she does, we will be ready for her.*

Vickie peeked out the windows again. *Are they armed? Two of them don't seem to be. But that man in the driveway has a huge sword. Will they come in? Do I tell my family what's happening? And how did they find me?*

That last question weighed the heaviest on her mind. She knew this was bad, but she couldn't make heads or tails of it.

The simple truth was that her admission into high school was enough for the Circle to find her. At the beginning of every school year, the administrators passed out school directories with the home numbers and addresses of each student.

The Circle simply requested one, to be collected at the school, and walked in pretending to be the father of one of the students there. It was a ruse that worked without difficulty and it provided exactly what they needed to know.

Vickie marched to the side door and opened it. "What do you want?"

Gabriel sneered. "It is not about what we want. It is about what the world needs. And this world needs to be free from the scourge of vampire rule. We thought it was over. But when you emerged, we knew. And now, we will work tirelessly to exterminate you."

"You can't come in here. I will kill all of you."

She could see a smile from under the hood, the torch-light bright on the lower part of his face. "That is precisely why we have been called to fulfill this great duty. It is time to put an end to the Age of Vampires once and for all. Enough is enough."

"I haven't done anything."

As she argued through the screen door, Craig rolled out of bed to see what all the commotion was about. "Vickie, what is it?"

"It's fine. I have it taken care of. Go back to sleep."

"It's two a.m. I won't go back to sleep. What is happening?" He looked out the window at the shrouded figure holding a torch in his back yard. Without missing a beat, he dialed nine-one-one.

"No, you can't do that. You'll only make things worse," she warned him.

"How can things get any worse, dear? They're here to kill you. That's as bad as it gets."

Seconds later, red-and-blue lights illuminated the street. When the Circle saw this, they were ordered by Gabriel to retreat but paused for a moment to issue a stern warning. "When the time comes, she will be stripped of her powers and she will be dead."

They hurried away through the back field, knowing it was vast enough that they could escape pursuit. Once there, they shoved their torches into the snow to extinguish them and raced away. "Don't drop anything," Gabriel ordered. "Everything you own has your DNA on it and they can track us. Keep a firm grip."

The cops barged into the house to see no evidence of anything having happened.

One officer sat at the kitchen table with Vickie to question her about the incident. "Were these people you knew?"

"Yes and no. I didn't know them, but I knew of them."

"Okay…and can you describe them?"

"They were of average height, but they were dressed in black robes with hoods over their heads. I couldn't see very much of their faces."

The officer continued to make notes. "The nine-one-one call indicated that they held torches. Is this correct?"

"Yes."

"Why would they do that?"

"You have to ask them, sir. I have no clue. I don't really know anything about this."

He flipped his notebook over. "But you said you knew of them."

"I knew of them, but I didn't know they would come to my home. I've never told them where I live."

"How would they have found you, then?"

"I don't know. That's the problem."

The officer began to get frustrated. *She has an answer for everything, it seems. But still, she doesn't know anything?*

"Did they threaten you? What kinds of things did they say?"

Vickie sighed. "They kept telling me they would kill me."

"For?"

"I don't know. I offered to talk to him and have the opportunity to plead my case although I didn't know what I was actually defending myself against. They weren't very clear."

"I'm sorry, miss, I have a hard time with this. I'll have to talk to your father."

To the officer's astonishment, Craig had the same answers that she did. No one knew what was going on, how to address it, or how to prevent it, only that an attack was threatened.

"Sir, can you think of any reason why this would have happened?

He shook his head. "Not at all. I don't understand it the least. But it happened. I saw it with my two eyes. Someone was on our property and issued threats against us. That much is certain."

"I don't know what we can look at, but I'll do my best to find more information pertaining to this case. It's possible that more groups resisted them, and probably for a good reason."

CHAPTER TEN

An old man named Wendell lived two doors down from the Watson household. A resident of the neighborhood since they first began building houses on that street in the 1980s, Wendell was rarely seen outside in the winter.

When the warm weather arrived, he was outside almost every day to mow his lawn in a large straw hat. Any time Alexis thought of him, she imagined that straw hat and his big white beard sticking out from under it.

The doorbell rang the next morning, and she saw the old man on the front porch when she pulled the door open. "Can I help you?"

"Is your father home, sweetheart?"

"Sure. One second." She stepped away from the door. "Dad! Door."

Seconds later, Craig walked through the living room on his way to the door. "Who is it?"

"I don't know. Some guy."

He looked out the front window. "Oh, hey, Wendell." He

pushed the front door open and stepped out onto the porch to greet his neighbor.

Alexis was taken aback. *That's Wendell? I didn't recognize him in that big coat and winter hat.*

Out on the front porch, the air filled with the cloudy vapor from the two men's breath. "What can I do for you, buddy?"

Wendell spoke in a calm, soft voice. "I wanted to stop by and make sure you were doing okay."

"Sure we are. What are you talking about?"

"My wife and I saw the police at your house late last night. The lights woke us up. We couldn't keep Cinnamon quiet. I'm surprised you didn't hear her."

He shrugged. *Cinnamon. That stupid, yippy little dog. The best part of winter is not having to hear that dog barking all day long in the back yard.* "Yeah, no, it was fine. Nothing major. It was a misunderstanding, that's all."

Wendell shook his head. "What kind of misunderstanding? Did someone make a mistake in calling the police?"

"Ah, no. I mean, yeah. I thought someone was trying to break into our house, so I called the cops. But there wasn't anyone there. It must have been my imagination or something."

"Oh, boy." The old man put his hands on his hips. "I tell you what, this neighborhood has had more problems in the last few years than I have ever experienced in my thirty plus years here. It's all going to garbage."

Craig feigned disgust with the direction of the neighborhood too and looked surreptitiously down the street from the front porch step. "I guess it's the way the world is going, Wendell. Sad, isn't it?"

"Oh, so sad." The old man looked at the step and shook his head. "I wish someone would come and clean it up. It could be so nice."

I need to wrap this up before anything slips out. "Okay, well, I should go in. I'm sorry if the lights woke you, Wendell. I didn't mean to disturb anyone else in the neighborhood." He slapped him on the shoulder.

"That's all right, Craig. I appreciate your concern. But I'm much more concerned that you are okay. If you ever feel the need to call the police, then do it. The rest of the neighborhood will understand."

He thanked the man and walked back into the house. *That was closer than I'd care to be with these things.* "Hey, girls! Come here for a sec. Family meeting."

They emerged from the back of the house and Vickie still rubbed the tiredness from her eyes. "What's up?" They both sat on the couch.

"We woke Wendell last night with our commotion. That means we need to be a little more careful. He asked more questions than I cared to answer about this situation."

Vickie folded her arms. "Okay, but I don't know how to stop these things from happening. If the Circle wants to strike, they will strike. What can we do to prevent them?"

Craig shook his head. "I don't know, but there has to be something. I don't want to be stuck in a situation where we give our secrets away to the rest of the neighborhood. We've been very lucky up to this point, and I want to keep it that way. I'll have to think of something."

"Does that mean we can't call the cops?" Alexis looked

confused. "We're stuck defending ourselves against whatever comes?"

He closed his eyes for a second. *She's right. This isn't something you can enforce. They need to have the freedom to call the police.* "Of course you can call the cops. But try not to let it be your first reaction, I guess. Entertain other possibilities first. Do what you can to solve the situation on your own." *You have no idea what you're saying. Stop there.*

After the talk, Vickie walked out the side door to the driveway. The wind howled and her teeth chattered while she huddled to keep warm. The snow swept off the large drifts next to the driveway and pelted her in the face while she walked around the garage to the field behind the house.

You're out there, somewhere. I know you're planning your next attack. We'll be ready for you—somehow.

She turned her head to the right and saw a large black line on the snow from where the escaping Circle members dragged their torches to put them out. Vickie walked up to the spot and stared down at it.

Where have I seen this before?

The vampire closed her eyes and scanned her memory for a moment that looked like that charred black spot. Before she knew it, she was back in her childhood again and stepped into that memory of hers.

Vickie stood outside the castle walls and looked at a burned portion of the ground. Lying beside it was an extinguished torch. She scanned the area until she saw Young Victoria approach the spot where she stood.

"Mutter! Vater! Come quick."

The girl's parents sprinted into view from the bottom

of a small hill. Again, she choked down a lump in her throat at the sight of them. *All I want to do is give them great, big hugs.*

They huddled around the black mark and the couple shook their heads in disappointment. "As if I don't have enough to fight right now." Her father sighed.

"What is it, Vater?" Young Victoria stood eagerly in front of him.

"Bad people." He sighed again as he turned to walk away.

Her dream self resumed her game while her parents shuffled back to the castle. Vickie could follow them and listen to their conversation.

"The last thing I need right now is a mob of people with torches and pitchforks interrupting my life." He shook his head with disgust. "I wish someone—anyone—would rein this all in and leave us alone. We're not Sangs!"

His wife placed her hand on his shoulder. "That's just it, though. We're trying to wake them up."

"You know, I fought Sangs last night. They warned me about something called Tyrhung."

My father fought the Sangs himself? I can't imagine him hurting a fly. Why didn't he ever talk about that?

"What does the Tyrhung do, darling?"

He raised his palms. "I'm not saying this is the truth. But some people have claimed that this sword is more powerful than anything else. No matter how much fight you bring to these people, the Tyrhung can do worse—and it usually does."

His wife was confused. "But you can tap into your

powers, right? You can duck and dodge it and overpower them?"

He pursed his lips in frustration. "No. This is not that kind of weapon. It finds you. If they wield the Tyrhung, they will win. Again, that's coming from a Sang I tried to kill, but I think you can believe it. He had no reason to lie."

The couple entered the castle, and Vickie followed closely.

"And you couldn't get through to any Sangs today, could you?"

The man shook his head. "No. They seem hellbent on destruction. I try to tell any of them who will listen that we can coexist with humans. But they want none of that. All they want to do is fight and kill them."

His wife sat in the large chair in the castle library. "And of course, the humans want to fight and kill the Sangs. And us."

"I won't stop fighting, though. I have to get this taken care of before it's too late. If I can defeat enough Sangs and convince them that we need to foster peace, we can avoid certain destruction. The way they talked about that sword, it might be the only weapon anyone needs to kill us. If we can't defend ourselves from it, we have nothing."

He sat on the sofa. She stood, walked to his side, and rested her head on his shoulder and her hand on his leg. "We will find the answer before it's too late."

"I don't want anything to happen to this family."

"I know. I don't either."

Vickie choked back more tears as she watched her parents show affection for each other in the midst of what must have felt like hopelessness. *If only they could have kept everything from happening. But I had no idea how tortured my father was about this entire situation.*

She snapped back to the present day in the field in the dead of winter and stared at the burned ground and melted snow.

Slowly, she shuffled back to the house, walked around the pool and through the back yard, and made her way to the driveway. One thing stood out strongly in her mind. *The sword can kill you, and it can negate your powers. If that's the same sword I saw them wield last night, it's no wonder they were so confident. They had it in the bag the second I saw them at the door.*

The vampire walked directly to her room and closed the door behind her. She laid down on her bed, her feet still on the floor, and stretched out. Nothing she thought about seemed to comfort her. She constantly envisioned ways to be killed over and over again. *I can't let myself be a victim. I am the last vampire. I want my bloodline to survive. It has to. And I can't let anything happen to my family, either.*

CHAPTER ELEVEN

"I've heard this movie is great," Jess blurted as the group power-walked through Mayfair Mall.

Near the back of the group, Vickie's gaze wandered around the two-story complex and she marveled at its sheer size. *This place is like a marketplace but way, way bigger.* She didn't have much time to drink it all in as they were almost late for the movie.

Vickie, Eric, Jess, Jamie, Alexis, and Will hurried through the mall on their way to see *Love is Blind,* a typical teen romantic comedy.

While the girls were all excited to see it and Vickie was thrilled to see her first movie in the theater, the boys seemed to have mixed reactions.

Will, for his part, didn't appear to look forward to it, but he never actually seemed to look forward to anything.

Eric was a little more vocal. "Yeah, we better hurry or we'll miss the previews for other lame chick flicks."

In mid-stride, Jess swung her arm back and slapped

him on the shoulder. "Shut up. You were outvoted this time. Deal with it."

"I'm always outvoted! Look around you—who else votes for good movies besides me?"

Alexis pumped her arms to pick up the pace. "Please hurry, okay? We'll pick one of your movies next time. We don't want to be late."

He rolled his eyes. *I've heard that one before.* "Oh, gee, yeah. If we're late, we might not be able to get a seat in the packed house."

Jamie giggled at his attitude, which caught Vickie's attention. *She really seems to like his humor. Look at that smile she gave him. Is that... Does she like him? I know everyone says no but come on. look at her.*

They finally reached the theater with a few minutes to spare. By then, the line wasn't too long, and they soon managed to buy their tickets at the counter.

"Okay, let's go," Alexis said to the group. "Theater nine. That's this way." She led them to the man who scanned their tickets and waved them through.

Vickie's eyes widened. "Is that all popcorn?"

Eric laughed. "Do they not have movie theaters in Austria or something?"

"Oh, well…uh, it's not that. I never really went to one. My family over there never took me."

He shook his head in disbelief. "You led such a sheltered life. Hey, movie theater popcorn is the best. Let's get a bucket. We can share it."

Alexis smiled and turned to Will. "Do you want to share a bucket with me?" She grabbed his arm.

He shook his head. "No, I'm not hungry. You can get one for yourself if you want."

Her smile faded. Behind them, Jess and Jamie both shook their heads. They knew Will was a lousy boyfriend, but no one could really convince Alexis of that.

After Eric bought a bucket of popcorn and a soda for them, they hurried down the hall to theater nine. When they walked in, he laughed at the turnout—three other couples sat near the front and the rest of the theater was empty.

"Oh, boy, thank goodness we got here early," he practically shouted. The girls all punched him in the arm. Jamie giggled again, which drew Vickie's stare.

They filed into a row and paired off in the luxury reclining seats. Will and Alexis went first, followed by Vickie and Eric, followed by Jamie and Jess. They all sank into the red leather and settled in. The previews began to roll.

Eric lifted the armrest between himself and Vickie and turned the reclining seat into a reclining loveseat. She smiled with wonder, and he put his arm around her. They leaned back cozily and placed the bucket of popcorn between them. *This is more like it. See? He likes you.* She breathed a sigh of relief. *He's showing you this much attention. Who cares about Jamie?*

On her right, Alexis unfortunately didn't have the same wonderful experience. Will insisted on keeping the armrest down so that he could be more comfortable. As the images flashed on the screen and lit up the theater, Vickie could see the annoyed look on her face.

Still, she had to enjoy her time with Eric. They could

snuggle and enjoy a movie together, and that was the most privacy they'd ever enjoyed up until that point. She smiled, satisfied with where she was.

A trailer was shown for a movie starring Tom Hanks. Eric whispered, "I love Tom Hanks. Such a great actor." Vickie gave him a blank stare. "*Forrest Gump? Apollo 13?* Nothing?" She shook her head. "Oh, man, we have some movies to watch. We'll have to hang out and watch Tom Hanks movies for a while."

"You won't hear me argue with that," she whispered in response.

Just then, Jamie leaned over. "Eric, do you remember that one we went to see where he played the retired rock star?"

He snapped his fingers, sat up, and smiled at her. "Oh yeah. And his drummer was the dude from *Dumb & Dumber*. That was a great movie."

"That was so funny!" She laughed and they high fived.

Eric leaned back again and slid his arm around Vickie. She glanced at Jamie, then at Eric, who was eating more popcorn. "Did you guys go see that movie as a group or something?"

He waved his hand vaguely. "Oh, no. Jamie and I saw it last spring. It was a good one."

She nodded, and her mind raced again. *They went to movies together? Just the two of them? What is everyone hiding from me? Maybe they actually dated for a while but they don't want me to know. Is everyone in on this? Alexis wouldn't lie to me about them, would she?*

As the opening credits to *Love is Blind* began to roll, he pulled her in closer, which temporarily calmed her mind a little. *Stop thinking and enjoy the movie. You're right where you want to be. This is all that matters.*

That attitude worked for Vickie during the movie, but when it was over, the thoughts rushed back relentlessly.

Alexis was the first to stand and she shoved her hands into her pockets. She didn't wear a smile and seemed disappointed by the whole experience. Will, clueless, stood and followed her.

The group walked out through the lobby and into the mall.

This gave Vickie an opportunity to look at the shops around them a little more. "How many stores are in here?" she wondered aloud.

Everyone looked at each other and shrugged. "A lot," Jess said. "Didn't you have malls in Austria, either?"

"Uh…not where I'm from, no."

"I want ice cream." Alexis was ready to drown her frustrations.

Jess and Jamie, both in tune with their friend, nodded in agreement. "Yes, but let's skip the ice cream place here." Jamie pointed to the big chain ice cream shop on the lower level of the mall below the movie theater. "I want Oscar's."

"Ooh, Oscar's!" Jess smiled. "Good idea."

"I can't go." Will hung back. "Sorry. I'll have to go home. That's okay, though. You all go."

Alexis sighed. "Fine."

The group gave the two of them a little space as they said goodbye to one another with a hug. Unfazed, Will turned and walked to the escalator while Alexis returned to the group. "Okay, let's go."

They started walking in the opposite direction to that

which Will had taken. Jess pulled her phone out. "I'll text my mom and let her know we'll walk to Oscar's."

Vickie released Eric's hand and hung back in the group to talk to Alexis. "Are you okay?"

"I'm fine."

"Are you sure? You don't look fine."

"I'll be fine after I eat some ice cream. Don't worry about it."

The friends walked out of the front entrance of the mall, across the parking lot, and turned left. Ten minutes later, they stood in front of a large black sign that read Oscar's Frozen Custard.

The bell above the door dinged as they all walked in. It was a busy Saturday evening for the shop, and they stood at the back of the long line and looked at the menu.

Eric nudged Jamie with his elbow. "Will you get the usual? Vanilla in a waffle cone?"

Jamie smiled. "That's the only way to fly. And let me guess, you'll order chocolate?"

"Of course. Anything else is a waste of time."

They both laughed. Vickie's face twisted in confusion over their continued rapport. Alexis noticed her expression. *Uh oh. She's getting jealous.*

Once they had all received their orders, they sat near a window looking out over the cold winter evening. Eric took a lick of his chocolate cone proudly. "Ah, Wisconsin. Where winter is as good a time for ice cream as any other time of year."

Jess smiled. "It's better. You're already cold anyway, so why not eat ice cream and think about warmer times?"

The booth seated three people on each side. Eric and

Vickie sat on one side, and the three other girls on the other. Jamie sat directly across from Eric, and the vampire continued to notice how often they made eye contact with each other.

Alexis caught her glance and tilted her head slightly as if to reassure her without actually saying the words. *It's okay. Don't worry about it. There's nothing romantic between them.*

But the vampire's emotions spiraled and she grew quieter as the evening wore on. By the time she had finished her cone, Eric leaned in and bumped her with his shoulder. "Hey, are you okay?"

"I'm fine." She didn't look at him.

"You seem very quiet, that's all."

She stuck out her bottom lip. "No, I'm fine. Really. I simply have nothing to talk about."

"Okay." His tone was unusually cautious. He knew something was wrong, but he didn't really have the courage to dig any deeper. In his mind, she was one step away from breaking up with him.

"There's my mom." Jess stood and pointed out the window at the van in the parking lot with its headlights on.

After they were dropped off at the house, Vickie caught Alexis by the arm as they walked in. "Hey, so what was your deal? Was it Will? Did he do something to you?"

Her sister rolled her eyes. "It's fine."

"No, it's not. I can tell you're not fine."

"I had really hoped we could snuggle up and enjoy the movie together. But that didn't happen. Instead, he simply sat there. He made no effort to have a good time. I just..." She shrugged.

"Why do you stay with him, then? There are other much nicer guys out there."

"No, there aren't. And he'll come around. I had hoped it would be faster, though. Besides, you have your own problems to deal with."

She recoiled in surprise. "What?"

"Oh, come on, Vickie. You're clearly bothered by Jamie. Look, I told you. They're only friends. They always have been. It's nothing for you to worry about so please, relax. She's not interested in him, and he has you now, so he's not interested in her. Forget about that."

Vickie walked past her on her way to her room. "It sure seemed like they have a lot of chemistry together."

"So what?" Alexis shrugged. "People can have chemistry and still not date. Jamie doesn't want to date Eric, and he would never cheat on you. I know both of those things as facts. Give it up. They're fine. You guys are fine. You had a great date. Why don't you simply enjoy it? At least one of us had fun tonight."

The vampire paused. *She's right. She had a terrible date and you're totally focused on worrying about your own stuff.* "Things will get better, Alexis. Really." *Once you leave the guy.*

"I know they will." She shuffled off to her room and shut the door, leaving her sister standing in the hallway. *I need to get Will out of this because all he's doing is hurting her.*

CHAPTER TWELVE

Vickie bounced on her heels in excitement while she stood in the entrance of the electronics store. *Oh, man. Look at all this great stuff.*

Eric stood behind her with his arms folded. "Are you ready yet?"

"Sorry, but I'm so excited! This is the first time I've had my own money to spend. I wanted to get something fun and tech-y."

He smiled as he put his arm around her, and they stepped forward into the store itself. "You're excited about gadgets? I wouldn't peg you as someone who was really into that sort of thing."

"Yeah, but that's because this is all so new to me. Seriously, look at those TVs over there. And there's stuff here I don't even know how to use or what it's for, but I want it for some reason."

He chuckled and shook his head. "I can't figure you out. Wouldn't Austria have some of these things? Like, you can't tell me you didn't have DVDs where you were."

"We did." *When I woke up.* "Um...my family didn't really load up on fancy stuff, that's all. We weren't a tech family. Most of this stuff might as well be brand new to me."

"Lead the way, then." He extended his hand. "This is your shopping trip. I'm only along to give you advice. My mom will be back in about an hour to pick us up."

She pumped her fist and strode off ahead of him, her gaze transfixed by all the different gadgets and devices she could see up and down the aisles. *This is a completely different world than what I have really ever seen.*

"Why do you look so surprised?" Eric asked. "You've been in this store before. You said Alexis and her dad brought you here to get a computer."

"They did, but her dad was so focused on getting a computer that we weren't allowed to walk around anywhere else. And I didn't really know what to expect, so I simply went with it." She turned left and walked down an aisle lined with fancy DSLR cameras and lenses. "Help me out—what are these for?"

"You...haven't seen a camera before?" *Where is Austria? In the Stone Age?*

"Oh! Sure. I guess I forgot." She laughed. "You know, everyone uses their phones now whenever they want to take pictures. I didn't remember that there was a separate device to do that." She picked up a display model and flipped it in her hands to inspect every angle of it with absolute fascination. "This is really big."

"Yeah. Cameras like that can get really big, especially if you slap on one of these lenses." Eric selected a lens that was more than half a foot long. "If you attach this to the front here, you can take pictures from really far away—or really close up. I have no idea what this one does."

"Hmm. It's cool, I guess, but if everyone has a phone that takes pictures, why would you lug this thing around? I don't understand."

He shrugged. "It depends on what you want to do. If you're fine taking normal photos, then yeah, your phone is good. But if you want to take more professional pictures, you'd need to go with something like this. These pictures are crisper and have better resolution."

Vickie raised her eyebrows but tried not to let her thoughts show on her face. *Alexis has a phone that takes pictures that are so clear, I think I could step into one. How do you get better than that?* "Maybe I'll pass."

They walked past a large stand with several rows of display phones. "What about a phone?" He pointed to the newest Google phones that were set up for demo. "I love these Pixel phones."

"You do?"

"Yeah. I'm not a big fan of Apple. Some people are, but I'm not. Google makes some cool phones. But I don't know how much money you have. These can be fairly expensive."

She picked up one of the display models and swiped the bright screen. "It's so sharp-looking. I'm not worried about the price, that part is fine. But I don't think Uncle Craig would be cool with me coming home with a phone."

"Why not?"

"He says I can't handle it yet. I don't know what he means by that."

"Maybe he wants you to get more used to living here

first. You've been here for like six months now, though, so maybe you're about ready."

Vickie wavered. *I really like this phone. It's so cool. And it would be a practical purchase. But I don't want to make anyone mad. I'll wait until he says it's okay.* "Let's look at some other stuff." She put the display unit back on its stand and continued her search.

A large stainless-steel box with doors on the front of it caught her eye and she stopped to stare at it. "Wow." She ran her fingers along the large handles and marveling at how smooth everything felt. "This is awesome. It's huge." Eric walked up behind her with a befuddled look on his face. "You know, if you're going to spend money, it's cool to get something that looks like you spent money. What do these little levers on the side do?"

He frowned although he had a smirk on his face. "They dispense ice and water. Vickie, this is a fridge. You're not buying a fridge."

"Oh. But it looks so fancy."

Eric leaned toward her. "Have you not seen a fridge before? How do you not know what this is?"

She raised her palms. "The only fridge I've really seen—or paid attention to, anyway—is the one at the house. And that one is, like, cream-colored and it looks nothing like this. It doesn't have the little water dispenser either."

He shook his head. *I'm starting to think she's not even from this world, much less this country.* "If you're worried that Mr. Watson will be upset with you for buying a phone, I can't imagine he'd be too thrilled with you buying a fridge. You already have a fridge, and this one is, like, seven hundred dollars. No high school girl should buy a full-size refrigerator."

The vampire nodded. "Okay, you're right. I didn't know what it was, that's all. Let's keep walking."

They meandered through a few different areas with items of varying interest. She was fascinated by the smart home devices but wasn't sure if she could bring those home. Drones were intriguing, but she didn't know what use she would have for them. And while she enjoyed the section with various electronic toys, Eric warned her not to bother with them.

But when they reached the home theater section, they both lit up with enthusiastic smiles.

"Now we're talking," he announced with glee as he stepped up to a wall full of high-definition screens. "Look at these 4K monsters. You know, TVs are a great buy—their prices are always coming down. It's a no-brainer."

"Really? Do you know a lot about TVs? I don't have one —except the one in the living room, of course."

He nodded. "Right, you don't have one of your own. These are cool. If you have the money, this is definitely the way to go."

Vickie gazed at the beautiful displays. A 4K video feed of hot air balloons drifted across all the TVs. "These pictures are so clear, I think I'm there. So, if I wanted to get one of these, which one would I get?"

Eric put his hands in his pockets and stretched his back. "That depends on what exactly you're looking for. Do you guys have cable?"

She scanned her brain for a second. "No. We don't have cable. My uncle thinks it's a rip-off."

"Cool. Then you want a smart TV. Most of these are, anyway."

"What does that mean?"

"It means it connects to the internet and you can stream all your shows and movies from there. And what's cool is that all these are flat, so you can hang it on your bedroom wall. It won't take up any extra space."

Vickie nodded as he made his case for the new TV. *No extra space means it won't be a big change. Having my own TV would be cool, I guess. No one will get mad at me for buying this, right?* "Let's get this one." She pointed to a 50-inch TV hanging on the wall.

Eric whistled. "A beauty. But holy cow—that's, like, four hundred and fifty dollars. Do you have that much to drop?"

"Yes. I want that TV."

"Okay, let me get a cart." He jogged to the front of the store.

As she milled about, waiting for him, a salesman in a bright blue polo shirt approached her. "Good afternoon, miss! Are you looking at our TVs?"

"Oh! Hi. Yeah, I'm buying this one."

"That's a great TV. One of our best sellers. You'll be very happy. And will you need anything else to go with it?"

She looked at the TV, then back at him. "Like what?"

"Where are you planning to put the TV?"

"In my bedroom."

"Okay, and you want to be able to watch it whenever you want, right?"

Where is he going with this? "Yeah..."

He waved her to follow him. "The last thing you want to do is bother anyone else in the house while you try to watch TV at night. And you also don't want to crane your neck to hear it because you have it so quiet either. What you need is a good pair of headphones."

The salesman led her to the relevant aisle, where she proceeded to try half a dozen different pairs. *I don't know what to choose. They're all great and every one of them sounds really good.* "What do you recommend?"

The salesman smiled, knowing he had her on the hook. He simply had to reel her in. "My advice would be that you go with something that will be comfortable to wear for long periods of time. That would be this pair—beautiful sound and they're very comfortable, and if anything, it'll sound better with these on than listening to the TV speakers." He selected a pair of high-end headphones and handed them to her. "Plus, they're Bluetooth, so you can connect to the TV wirelessly."

Vickie placed the headphones over her ears and was immediately astounded. *These are so comfortable. I could wear these all night.* "I'll take them."

He nodded, his expression smug. "Why don't you go meet your friend over there? I'll get this and your TV and ring it all up."

A confused Eric waited in the TV section and looked in every direction for her. "Geez, I thought I lost you. Where were you?"

She pointed behind her. "That nice man told me that I needed headphones."

"For what?"

"To listen to the TV at night."

He came up to them and loaded the TV and the box of

headphones onto the cart Eric brought over. Her boyfriend's mouth dropped.

"Vickie…those are three-hundred-and-fifty-dollar headphones."

She looked off into the distance as she did the math in her head. "That's fine."

Fine? Are you serious, girl?

The salesman nodded and positively beamed with enthusiasm. "The total comes to $808.41, with tax and everything."

Vickie slid her hand into her pocket and withdrew eight hundred dollars in cash. "Shoot. I'm a few dollars short."

"That's okay. Let me see if I can get you a discount of some kind so we can swing the deal in your favor." He tapped his keyboard a few times. "I was able to get you an extra five percent off, so that knocks forty dollars off the price, and you can cover the purchase in cash."

"Perfect." She handed the money over, took the change, and led Eric to the main entrance.

They stood inside the vestibule where they waited for Eric's mom to arrive. "I can't believe you dropped eight hundred dollars like that."

"Why not? It's my money. I earned it, I should be able to spend it, right?"

CHAPTER THIRTEEN

The bell rang seconds after Vickie made it to general business class, literally in the nick of time.

She had been exhausted all day thanks to her new purchase. Craig didn't respond when she walked in with a new TV and expensive headphones. He was worried that he would have to help her set it up, but Alexis took care of that.

"This is so cool. I'll be in here all the time." She repeated that constantly as they set the TV up while he sat in his chair in the living room and simply shook his head.

He was amused by her impulsiveness but thought she would ask him to mount it on the wall so she wouldn't have to buy an actual wall mount. Their solution was to place it on top of her dresser.

Craig walked past the room as the girls set it up and logged into the family Netflix account. *That TV seems bigger than the one we have in the living room. What does she need that for? Sheesh. She'll miss having the entire top of her dresser now that it's covered with that thing.*

"Now, Vickie, we'll have to set some rules here. You can't watch this TV while you're doing homework, for one."

"Of course." She was too excited to really pay attention to what he said.

"And when you go to bed, this stays off. You have to get up in the morning, and I don't want to see your schoolwork suffer because you have a TV in here."

"No problem." She still wasn't listening.

That night, after he went to bed, she stayed up until two a.m. watching her TV. Alexis helped her pair the Bluetooth headphones with the set. And since they were so comfortable, she simply laid in bed and watched old episodes of *The Office*. She didn't understand half the jokes, but she didn't care. It looked beautiful in her room.

The real challenge, however—even for a vampire—came when she had to drag herself through the halls the next day. It was also the reason why she was almost late to general business class.

Mr. Numerich saw her rush in, and he raised his thumb and index finger. "This close, Hewitt."

"Yes, sir. Sorry!" She took her seat as he stood to speak to the students.

"Class, we will start our semester-long project today. You will pair off into teams of two. I will hand out these papers. Please take one and pass it around, and I will walk through it with you. But before I do that, let's pair off into groups."

Of course, he wouldn't allow the students to choose for themselves. He had gone ahead and decided the teams beforehand, and he merely had to formally announce them to the class.

To the vampire's delight, she was paired off with April Kyle.

She was a nice enough girl, seemed friendly, and always sat near Vickie. April remained quiet, and she was a studious girl. *This is great. Someone who won't slack and might keep up with me.*

The girl stood, moved to the seat immediately beside Vickie, and greeted her with a smile. "I guess we'll be roomies."

"I guess so." She returned the smile but laughed inwardly. *What does roomies mean?*

Mr. Numerich handed a stack of papers to one of the kids seated in the front of the class, who took one and passed them back. Once the pile reached Vickie and April, the vampire took one and handed them to the student closest to her.

She glanced at it. On one side of the sheet was a list of categories, like Rent, Automobile, Groceries, and others. On the right side of the sheet were empty boxes.

"These are your budgets." The teacher craned his neck. "In this project, you and your partner are independent adults. You no longer have classes. You no longer have homework. You are out in the real world, as they say. What you will do is create a budget for your spending that will be realistic and doable for yourselves as roommates. This means that you must decide how to split the budget, who pays for what, and so on."

Mike Arroyo raised his hand. "How do we know how much this stuff costs?"

"That's the assignment. You will do the research and find an apartment that fits your budget, as well as an internet plan, an entertainment streaming service perhaps, and anything else you want to pay for."

Vickie raised her hand. "Why do we do this?"

He smiled. "It is very important for you to understand how to spend your money."

"But...don't you simply go to the store and give it to someone?"

The teacher laughed a big belly laugh—one that was louder than anything else he had done in the class to that point. "Yes, but that is also a quick way to spend all your money."

"Can't you make more of it?"

He raised his hand. "All right, let's leave it there for now. You'll get the idea as we go along, okay?"

Another kid raised his hand. "How do we make these budgets if we don't know how much money we make?"

With a glint in his eye, Mr. Numerich stepped over to his desk, reached underneath it, and withdrew a large black top hat. "Your jobs are in here. You will all draw a piece of paper from this hat. There are various jobs included here, and the salary will be noted on the paper as well. All you have to do is draw a piece of paper and that will be your job—and paycheck—for the semester. Now, who would like to go first?"

One by one, the students drew papers from the hat, and the jobs included things like plumber and librarian. A couple of kids hit the jackpot and drew things like investment banker and CEO of a multinational corporation.

Mr. Numerich reached the back of the room, where Vickie and April waited for their turn.

The vampire reached into the hat, felt around, and pulled out a slip of paper. *Bank teller? What's a bank teller? And it only makes eleven dollars an hour?*

Once all the slips of paper were dispersed, the students were then tasked to come up with apartments that would fit in that budget.

April smiled as she held her slip of paper up. "I'm a marketing associate. I make fifty thousand dollars a year. Score!"

They pulled their calculators out and estimated their take-home paychecks after the tax rate that was listed on the budget form for reference. "I'll only take home about three hundred and forty dollars a week, or one thousand three hundred and sixty dollars a month."

"Perfect." April scooted forward a little. "And I'll take home about three thousand dollars a month after taxes."

"Wow, you'll make twice as much as me."

The girl waved her hand airily. "Whatever. It was the luck of the draw." She used both hands to tighten the ponytail that held her long, light brown locks out of her face. "Where should we live?"

Vickie located a sheet of apartment listings Mr. Numerich provided. "Look at this one—two bedrooms, and it has a fireplace, a community pool, central air, and a balcony overlooking Lake Michigan."

April shook her head. "Yeah, right. It's also one thousand five hundred dollars a month."

"So what?" The vampire looked at her, a little confused.

"If we split it, that still leaves us with money left over. Or you could pay more of it since you make more."

"Uh…that's not fair, Vickie. Look, I don't want to spend that much on rent right out of the gate. It sounds like a nice place, but there are some here that are more in the six-hundred-dollar range."

She studied them quickly. "They don't sound as cool as that other one."

"Right, but that's the point. We can't simply get what we want. We're supposed to learn to get what we need. Otherwise, we'll run out of money in no time."

After a little discussion, they finally agreed on a two-bedroom duplex in West Allis. April laughed. "Living in 'Stallis isn't ritzy, but it's affordable. And besides, there are so many things to do there." It took Vickie a moment to remember that the word 'Stallis was often used in place of West Allis.

"Okay, class, I won't pass out your checkbooks. These are registers that you will use to track your income and your expenses. It is a good exercise for those who need to learn more in practical terms."

Mike Arroyo raised his hand again. "But there are apps and services that track your money for you. Why bother with a paper checkbook? Shouldn't all this stuff be done online?"

Mr. Numerich raised his finger. "Ah! Class, Mr. Arroyo here has asked a very important question. Why learn this if there are apps that can do it for you? And that is something I can understand. Today's apps can generate reports and give you all kinds of insight into your finances with only a few clicks. However, that is not what we are here to learn."

He stepped to his left and looked at the tops of the desks in front of him. "I am teaching you the concepts and principles necessary to build a better financial life for yourself. This is not simply about knowing how and when to spend money. You are also here to learn why you spend money. To learn about your financial habits. These are very important lessons to learn, and they are why I teach this class in the first place. It would be very easy of me to say, 'Go download Mint and everyone gets an A-plus.'"

The students laughed. "But that's not the point here. The point is that you need to know what these apps actually do for you. Yes, they do the math, but it's important that you know how to do the math as well. You need to know how to balance your checkbook regularly and how to make it work for you. Everyone thinks a little differently, and that is what we are trying to discover here."

April shrugged. "It makes sense."

But Vickie, who had grown a passionate love for all things tech-related, was totally bummed. *I used to write with pencil and paper or whatever all the time when I was younger. I want to use apps—why not take advantage of technology while it's here?*

Still, she wasn't one to make waves and especially not with this particular teacher. Instead, she kept her head down and worked hard, even if it didn't always make sense to her.

CHAPTER FOURTEEN

While Vickie slept that evening, she had a very vivid dream.

She stood in an empty field with tall, green grass blowing in the wind. The sky was bluer than she had ever seen in her life, and the sunshine baked her skin and filled her with a warmth she had never felt before.

She closed her eyes, looked at the sun, and inhaled deeply. After exhaling, she opened her eyes and her knees almost buckled.

Standing before her were her parents.

Her mother, her hands folded in front of her, wore an exasperated look of relief at seeing her daughter. A gray streak highlighted her dark hair that blew around her slightly wrinkled face. Her father simply stood with his arms at his sides, a relaxed smile on his face.

She wanted to run to them, but she couldn't move from her spot in the field. "Mutter? Vater? Is this another vision?"

"No, my daughter. This is not a memory." Her father waved her over. "Come with us."

Vickie looked down at her feet. "I…I can't. I can't move. I want to be near you. Please."

"It's okay." Her mother spoke calmly. Even though the wind was howling, Vickie could hear their voices clearly. "We want you to come with us where it is safe. You are under attack."

"I know. I want to go with you. But…I don't want the legacy of the vampire to be what it is now. These people don't know who we are. They don't know what we were. The world sees us as no different from the Sangs."

He nodded. "Victoria, right now, you are no different from the Sangs."

"What does that mean?"

"Come with us. Please. Or you will have to fight."

Vickie's lip quivered. "I don't know if I can."

Her mother laughed. "Of course you can, my daughter. You are still a vampire. This has not changed."

"I know, but I can't simply…I can't fight. I can't fight them the way I need to. And I certainly can't fight them if they have that sword with them."

Her father's eyebrows raised. "They have the sword?"

"Yes, Vater."

He nodded. "You will face that sword. If they have it, at some point, it will be your turn."

She shook her head. "But I don't want to die yet. I'm building a life here now."

"Then you will need someone to watch your back. Someone who can help you when you are at your lowest point."

"Who? What do you mean by that? Why are you speaking like this?"

Her parents looked at one another and her father nodded. "We have to go."

"No! Please" She reached out with both arms, desperate to clasp her parents and hold onto them. But they were out of arm's reach, and she still could not move her feet.

Her eyes snapped open. She lay in her bed, her headphones still on her ears. On the TV, Dwight fumed at Jim and Pam for putting his office supplies in the vending machine. The glow of the TV nearly blinded her. *Ugh. I should have turned this off. I don't even know what's going on.*

She grabbed the remote and turned it off, pulled the headphones off her ears, and tossed them on the nightstand. As she brushed her hair out of her eyes, her stomach twisted.

Oh no. Not again.

Vickie looked at her window and saw the faint orange glow. *They're back.*

The vampire bounded out of her bed, sprinted into Craig's bedroom, and shoved him a few times to rouse him.

"Wh...huh?" Craig moaned and scowled at whoever had interrupted his slumber.

"They're back. The Circle is back."

He sat up. "Are you sure?" he whispered. She nodded. "Okay, give me a second. No cops. For now, stay quiet."

The sound of her running through the hall had jostled Alexis awake, who stumbled out into the hallway. "Hello? What's going on?"

The vampire ran back into the hallway to stop her sister. "Shh. The Circle is here again."

"What will you do? We can't call the cops again."

"I know. Your dad is on it."

Alexis shook her head at the idea. *What can my dad do? It's not like he's some talented fighter. The guy is no match for them.* "We need to call the cops," she contradicted herself.

"We can't." Vickie tried to whisper while she grasped Alexis' shoulders. "There's too much attention on this house already."

Craig emerged from the bedroom in a t-shirt and pair of sweatpants and held his fully loaded shotgun at his side.

"Dad?" His daughter looked stunned. "You have a gun?"

He nodded. "I've had this for a while. I know how to use it, too. Let's get rid of these jerks."

"What do you want me to do?" the vampire asked.

"Go to the side door and talk to the leader. Get his name. Get any information you can. I'll get into position at the living room window. There's a hole in the screen that I planned to fix in the summer. But if you talk to him, you can distract them all long enough for me to open the window and get ready."

Alexis grabbed him by the shoulder. "Dad...you won't kill them, will you?"

He looked her in the eyes, his expression grim. "I don't know. I don't want to, and I don't plan on it. But if they come in here and try to hurt or kill either of my girls, they take their lives into their own hands. Stay back. When you hear the first shot, get Vickie away from the door and you two huddle in the hallway."

"What if they have guns, too?"

"I think they would have fired them by now. They have a big sword, that's all. But either way, stay in the hall."

Vickie eased the side door open slowly. Gabriel stood in the driveway and again held the sword in one hand and a torch over his head with the other.

"You are the last vampire, and you must be exterminated," he intoned coldly when he saw her.

"I won't step out of this house. What is your name?"

She'll be dead soon, anyway. What difference does it make? "I am Gabriel, the leader of the Circle and a direct descendant of those who rid the world of vampires. Your demon-filled days are over. Your time of feasting on the flesh of the human race has come to an end."

She raised her eyebrows. "I'm honestly not sure what you're talking about there. I don't do any of that stuff."

He gritted his teeth. "You are the last descendant of the vampire race. By blood, you do these things. I know it for a fact."

"You have your facts wrong."

Craig tiptoed slowly and carefully through the living room. The curtains on the wide windows were closed so he couldn't be seen from the outside. *I always hated these curtains, but they're saving my life now. Thanks for choosing those, Carol.*

As quietly as possible, he dragged the couch a few inches away from the window and gave himself enough room to slide in and position himself. He dropped to his knees and held his breath as he lifted the sash to expose the torn screen.

He clenched his jaw as he slid the barrel of the shotgun through the hole and aimed it at Hannes, who trembled in the front yard. *There you go. I have a clean shot on this guy. Now, wait for the right moment.*

"Enough of these questions," Gabriel protested impatiently. "We are not here for anything other than your demise."

With the window open, he could hear the man talking from the living room. *What is this guy on? No one talks like that.*

He squeezed the trigger and the shot clipped Hannes in the shoulder. "I'm hit," he shouted and immediately dropped the torch into the snow, where it hissed as it extinguished.

Craig's heart raced as he shifted to his left and aimed the barrel toward the driveway where the next man would undoubtedly appear. Another torch-bearing figure moved, and he fired, although this time, he struck the dirt in front of him.

Regardless, the message had been received. At the side door, Gabriel took his eyes off his quarry to see what had happened. Vickie saw this as her opening, tapped into her super-speed, and threw the side door open. She launched herself into him, hurled him back across the driveway, and followed to punch the wind out of his lungs. As he gasped for breath, she saw the sword on the ground.

She picked it up and immediately began to shake. Her eyes wide, she dropped the blade and turned to sprint into the house, but her legs wouldn't kick into her super-speed. Instead, she jogged slowly to the door, closed it quickly, and locked it behind her.

Still sprawled on the cold earth, Gabriel smiled at her reaction to the sword. He pushed himself to his feet, retrieved his weapon, and made his way to the front of the house.

When he turned the corner, Craig fired another shot, but this one bounced off the blade.

"There is too much noise which will draw too much attention. We must go." The leader gestured for his team to follow, and they sprinted to the field again. This time, however, Hannes moved much slower and clutched his shoulder the entire way.

"They're gone," Vickie announced but kept her gaze focused on their retreat in case they turned back. "Thank you so much."

"Are you okay?" Craig walked over and put his hand on her shoulder.

"Yeah. I just…feel funny. There really is something evil about that sword. It sapped me of my power for a second there."

Alexis nodded as she walked into the kitchen. "And that explains why they were able to kill so many vampires and Sangs. Wow."

"It was scary. But I'm glad it's over now."

"It is. For now." He walked to the window and looked out at the night sky. "I wish I could have taken some better shots. Man. Anyway, I have to lock this up because the police will be here eventually."

"So what?" His daughter shrugged. "You have a license for that, don't you?"

"Of course. But if the cops come, they'll ask any number of questions, and I don't want to risk any more of this. I want to be able to say, "Hey, we don't know where that came from. Sorry."

Craig hurried down the hallway, unloaded his gun, and packed it away under his bed. He ran back to the kitchen. "Girls, get to bed. We'll play dumb when the cops arrive. Nothing happened, no one fired any guns, and we don't know what anyone is talking about. They're crazy, not us." *I wish I could believe that myself.*

Sure enough, the police arrived on their doorstep within a few minutes. Craig answered the door and tried to look as groggy as possible while he firmly denied that there were any torches or any guns fired from their property.

Once the police were gone, he breathed a sigh of relief. *Another bullet dodged. I don't know how many more of these I can pull off.*

As he walked down the hall, Vickie opened her bedroom door and met him in the hallway to wrap her arms around him. "Thanks."

He patted her on the head. "Of course. No one messes with my family and gets away with it. That's why I got the gun in the first place. Now, try to get some sleep. And for crying out loud, keep that TV off for the rest of the night."

She smiled. "You got it." She returned to her room and crawled into bed where she forced herself to relax and exhaled loudly. *I still don't know how to sleep after something like that. Goodness. At least I'm safe for tonight. But I wish I knew what my parents were talking about in that dream.*

CHAPTER FIFTEEN

After all the drama of the night before, the adrenaline that still coursed through her body when she went to bed was too much for real relaxation. Vickie didn't sleep much, but she wasn't too concerned about it.

All she could think about was how Craig—her new father or uncle, depending on what company she was in—had stepped up and saved her from certain death.

She got out of bed at five thirty a.m. and headed to the kitchen, trying not to make too much noise. *I've watched them do this stuff a hundred times now. I even helped Alexis do it once. I know what to do on my own.*

The vampire took a package of bacon and a carton of eggs out the fridge and placed two pans on the stovetop. *Let's see...they have little pictures to show which burner goes to which knob. There we go.* She turned one of the burners to medium heat and threw in some bacon.

While that began to simmer, she mixed eggs in a bowl. That was when Craig stumbled down the hall to see what she was doing.

"What's going on?" He yawned and rubbed his eyes. "Why do I smell bacon already?"

"Oh! Good morning." She gave him a warm smile. "I decided to make breakfast."

He blinked a few times. "Am I still sleeping?"

She giggled. "No, really, I'm making breakfast. Eggs, bacon, and toast."

"What for? You have school today. You don't have to do this."

Vickie nodded. "I know. But I wanted to find a way to say thank you for protecting me last night."

"Oh. Don't worry about that."

"No, really. Listen…" She gestured for him to have a seat while she turned the burner on for the eggs. "Do you want to know what my last memory of my father was?"

"What's that?"

She turned and leaned up against the counter, the spatula in hand. "He scooped me up in his arms and ran as fast as he could—well, without revealing himself, obviously—to our home. He didn't say anything and simply ran."

"From what?" Craig rested his elbows on the table.

The vampire stared off into space. "I don't know. He never really said. Looking back now, I assume it was probably the Circle, but he wouldn't say at the time. All he wanted to do was get me safely into the castle." She turned to pour the eggs into the pan.

"You need to spray that pan first. There's cooking spray in the cupboard up and to your left."

She caught herself before the eggs poured out of the bowl. "Oh, thanks. Whoops!"

"It's okay."

"Anyway, he was determined to get me into that castle and behind those doors. It was the only thing on his mind. He didn't think and he didn't explain but simply acted. My father knew that, for some reason only known to him and my mother, I was in danger. And he took care of it." She sprayed the pan and her nose wrinkled, then poured the eggs in. They sizzled too. "Boy, cooking can get loud."

He chuckled. "Yeah, it can, depending on the meal. Bacon and eggs do a fair amount of sizzling. So, why are you telling me this about your father?"

Vickie stirred the scrambled eggs in the pan, set the spatula on the counter, and turned to look at him. "For four hundred years, I lived in a box with no light, no contact with anyone else, no movement...nothing. All I had were my memories. But you probably know, too, that the last memory you have of someone is always the clearest. It's the one you associate with that person forever, right?"

He nodded. "Often, that's the case, yes."

"The last memory I have of my father is of someone who protected me. He watched over me. When I was in danger, he didn't think twice about his own safety. He took action and saved me."

"Okay."

"Last night, you did the same thing."

Craig tilted his head and frowned slightly. "Well, I wouldn't say that. I simply—"

"No, no, hear me out." She interrupted him and he didn't protest. "Because of who my father is and what he did for me, I've thought that the perfect father is one who protects his kids. That's what my dad did for me. Last night, all I had to do was tell you that the Circle was here.

You didn't think twice about it. You stepped in, took action, told everyone what to do, and marched into harm's way to get rid of them."

He took a breath. "Well, sure. Why wouldn't I do that? They were trespassing, making threats…anyone would've done that."

"No, they wouldn't have. It takes an honorable man to do that, especially for someone who isn't technically his daughter." She turned away to check the bacon. "I don't know…one of the hardest parts of being alive now is the fact that my parents are gone. They were my protectors and always watched out for me. Especially my dad. Last night was the first time since I woke up that I felt like I was safe. Like I was taken care of."

"I'm glad you felt that way. I want you to feel that way here. You're here and you're family. And as far as the United States Government is concerned, you're blood family." He winked.

She laughed. "I know bacon and eggs isn't that big a gesture for people who have eaten it their whole lives, especially as a thank you for someone who took up arms to defend me, but—"

"Hey, I don't want to hear it. Bacon and eggs is always a fine gesture. Besides, it's the thought that counts, and I know this is a big deal for you. So I appreciate the gesture as much as you appreciate what happened last night." Craig stood from the table, walked over, and gave her a hug. He looked over her shoulder. "But you'd better get those eggs off the burner. They're more than done."

His daughter stumbled through at precisely the right

moment, and the three of them sat and ate breakfast together as a family.

"This feels weird." Alexis chuckled as she took a bite of bacon. "It feels like a Sunday morning breakfast or an I'm-bored-during-a-summer-morning breakfast. I'm not used to having a nice hot meal on a school day."

"Don't get used to it." He smiled as he took a sip of orange juice. "This only happens when I take up arms. I definitely don't plan to do that every night."

She shook her head. "I can't believe you have a gun and you didn't tell me."

"I wasn't hiding it, not really. I only wanted to make sure that...well, you would be okay with it."

She stabbed a mouthful of eggs with her fork. "I think I'm more impressed that you're such a good shot."

The girls laughed while he hung his head. "If I was a good shot, we'd have three dead guys on our lawn this morning. I'm not that good."

The school day was uneventful—something Vickie was grateful for considering how tired she was. By the time she made it to the library, Tricia sat at their usual table and scribbled frantically on a piece of notebook paper.

"Hey, why are you being so crazy right now?" She dropped her bag on the chair next to her as she sat.

"Oh, this paper is due in the next hour and I need to have it done before then. I've tried to squeeze time in during my other classes, but it's been tough today."

She was surprised. "Why didn't you do it at home?"

Tricia looked up from her paper with a smile. "You're adorable."

"What?"

"Come on. I don't want to do schoolwork at home. That's why you go home—to get away from school. And I didn't have time to do it last night. My boyfriend came over."

Vickie leaned forward to see the assignment she was working on. "It looks like a long paper. When was it assigned?"

"Last week."

"You had a whole week to do it? What did you do this weekend?" *How do you have a whole week to work on something and you're still not done? That's really irresponsible.*

The girl laughed. "I wasn't exactly in any condition to do homework if you know what I mean."

The vampire narrowed her eyes in confusion. "I…don't know what you mean."

Tricia looked around in disbelief. "Wow, how much of a goody-two-shoes are you?" When her companion continued to stare in confusion, she explained patiently. "Look, I had a couple of bottles of wine at my house over the weekend. That's simply how it goes, you know? Have you never had a drink?"

After the last drink I had, I was unconscious for four hundred years. "No, drinking's not really my thing."

"Good for you. You probably have a good home life, hey? Good parents?"

"Um…yeah. The best."

"Yeah, see, I don't have that so much. I have trouble with my dad and drinking is far better than dealing with him. And my mom is the one who brings the wine in, so…" She shrugged.

Vickie's stomach sank. *She has a terrible household. She needs help. What can I do for her?* "Do you want to stay at my house for a little while?"

Tricia looked out of the corner of her eye. "For what?"

"You know, until we can figure out what to do next?"

Her friend put her pen down. "What are you talking about?"

She leaned in and whispered, "You can't drink to escape a bad home life. You need to get help. I don't know what I can do for you, but at least that would be a start."

"Vickie, you're great." Tricia gave her a smile of pity. "You're so sweet. Thank you. But I'm fine. I don't need anything. This is simply how my life is."

The vampire leaned back in her chair. "But if you are always rushing and late with your assignments, you won't do very well in school."

"Sister, I have news for you. I don't do very well in school and never have. Besides, you would be surprised what you can talk your way out of if you have the right charm with the right teachers. I can get extensions on anything."

"Really?"

"Oh yeah. Tell 'em your grandpa died or something. It doesn't matter what you say to them, as long as you can fake it well enough. That's the key. Oh, and bonus points if you can cry. I can usually muster up some tears here and there, but only if I think they're not buying my story. Shoot, this paper I'm working on? It was due last Friday. I bought myself half a week by telling Mrs. Curtis that the power was out at my house."

"Wow. I had no idea. That's a lot of lying, isn't it?"

Tricia shrugged. "In my mind, it ain't lying if someone believes it. And if it gets you a little leeway with the teachers, great. I think that's the only way I'll get through school."

She lowered her head and continued to write frantically on her paper. Meanwhile, Vickie was astounded by everything she had learned about her new friend.

I can't believe this. She has a terrible relationship with her parents. She drinks. She doesn't do homework at home. She lies to her teachers. How much of this is her having a rough life but meaning well, and how much of this is merely her being a bad person?

Not wanting to stare at her in disbelief, Vickie pulled her math homework out and opened it. *I don't know if I can concentrate on any of this, but at least I won't weird her out. I don't know what to say to her. Do I say anything? Or do I leave it as is? Or am I simply the naive one here?*

CHAPTER SIXTEEN

That weekend, the two girls lounged in Vickie's room and watched *The Office* on the big TV.

Vickie laughed at *Date Mike* while Alexis swiped continuously on her phone.

"You know, sometimes, I get annoyed at that phone." The vampire shook her head.

"What?"

"You're always on there lately. I know you're not texting with Will. Is there really that much to look at on Facebook?"

The other girl laughed. "There's always something to do on Facebook. Come on, now."

She sighed. "I'm enjoying the new TV, but I'm bored. Does Facebook really entertain you that much?"

"It's something to do." She slipped her phone into her pocket. "Our friends can all keep up with each other. Plus, I have, like, two hundred and fifty friends on there. Someone's always on. If there's nothing else going on, we play games or whatever."

"Can I get on Facebook? Why haven't we set me up on there yet?"

Alexis pointed to her. "Funny you should mention that. When you first came over here during the summer, I asked my dad about it. Because, you know, all my friends are on it and we talk all the time. I thought it would be a good way to get you…acclimated, I guess. Everyone else is on Facebook, so you could be too."

"What did he say?"

"He said we should wait because there are so many privacy issues on Facebook, and he didn't want you to make any mistakes that could out you as a vampire, that sort of thing. It was all about 'Let's get her situated here first before we do something like that.'"

Vickie looked out the window at the falling snow. "I think I'm situated. I've been here for a long time now. I have a boyfriend. What else do we need?"

Alexis shrugged. "Let's go ask him."

She laughed when she walked in on her father, who was already falling asleep in his chair in the living room. His eyes snapped open when he realized the girls stood in front of him.

"Ladies. What can I do for you?" He shifted his weight to straighten in the chair.

"Dad, Vickie wants to be on Facebook."

You knew this would happen eventually. "Ahhhh…I don't know."

"What are you worried about?" The vampire shook her head. "I've taken much better care of myself. I don't take as many risks as I used to. Come on, this is the perfect time. Besides, I'm bored out of my mind."

Craig stared at her, then at his daughter, then back to her again. "Fine. But Alexis, keep an eye on her there. Make sure she stays safe and doesn't do anything foolish."

"Got it, Dad. Come on, Vickie, let's get your laptop."

They ran down the hall and into the bedroom. Vickie flipped the laptop open and went to Facebook's web site. In a few minutes, they had created a profile and uploaded her picture.

"I messaged my friends and told them to friend you when they have a chance, so you should get a flood of requests in soon."

"I'm excited." She bounced on the bed. "Your dad said I shouldn't do anything foolish. What did he mean? What should I do? Or not do?"

"Okay, so first, don't accept any friend requests from people you don't know."

She was confused. "Why would I do that?"

"Some people do." Such an innocent question was refreshing to Alexis. "There seriously are people who care only about getting their numbers up, or whatever. It's stupid. They want to have so many friends so they feel popular or something. Do your best to keep to friends who are actually your friends. Don't worry about your numbers."

"Okay. That seems easy enough." Vickie assumed using Facebook responsibly simply meant using common sense.

But according to Alexis, there wasn't much common sense in the Facebook world. "You'd be surprised how often people get hacked there. Don't click on anything you don't recognize. Don't open any messages from anyone you don't know. Never send your password to anyone."

Her tone of voice was far more annoyed than concerned or serious.

"You sound like this whole thing bothers you."

"Not really, but…it doesn't take much to really stay safe on Facebook. Seriously. But there are so many people who do dumb stuff and ruin it for the rest of us. No one should ask you for your password and no one should ask you for any personal information. Okay? Only deal with people you trust and filter out the rest."

Vickie leaned back on her pillow and stared at the screen, which now popped with red notifications of new friend requests. "It sounds like Facebook doesn't have to be so scary. How did it get this way?"

"Old people." Alexis laughed and shook her head. "It's all the old people on it. Me and my friends don't really want to be on Facebook, but it's the only real social media that has enough stuff for us to do. That's why we stay."

She dragged her finger across her trackpad. "Should I accept these requests, then?"

"Yeah, if you know who they are."

One of the first requests on the list was from Eric. Vickie smiled. *I know this one.* She clicked on *Accept* and immediately received a message from her boyfriend.

Eric: **Well, well! Looks who's on Facebook**

Vickie: **Yay! Alexis got me logged on**

Eric: **Finally! Now I don't have to call your dad's phone or Alexis's phone to talk to you. We can chat on here**

Vickie: **I didn't even think of that. This is so nice. I guess her dad didn't want me on here**

Eric: **I suppose he was only worried about you. He seems like a good dad/uncle**

Vickie: **He really is. I know he thinks about my safety, that's all**

Alexis laughed when she saw Vickie chatting intently on her laptop, ignoring the giant TV in front of her face. "Welcome to social media, girl. You're sucked in now."

Out in the living room, Craig squirmed in his chair. *There's something about this that makes me really uncomfortable. Should she be on Facebook yet? Can she handle it? She's gone a few months without doing anything too revealing, but if she slips up on there, it's over.*

He pulled his phone out and searched for articles about *Facebook dangers.*

Like any internet search, he was immediately inundated with horror story after horror story of kids who were lured away, kidnapped, or worse simply by using Facebook irresponsibly.

He stood hastily and knocked on Vickie's door.

"Yeah?"

He opened the door and poked his head in. "Vickie, a quick word of warning. You know how, when you slipped up in public and revealed yourself, we had to swoop in and kinda cover for you?"

"Uh huh."

"If you slip up on Facebook, it's way worse. There's a public record of it, and it can be saved by other people. We can't save you if something bad happens on Facebook. Okay? So please, whatever you do, be careful. And never click on anything—"

"That I don't recognize. Yep, I already had that speech from Alexis."

Craig looked at his daughter, who stared at him and clicked her tongue. "Okay, then. I want you to have fun on there, but I don't want you to get yourself in trouble, that's all."

"Don't worry, Dad, I have a feeling she'll mainly use it to message her boyfriend anyway."

"Shut up. I'll do other stuff." Vickie threw a pillow at her sister, who ducked and laughed.

"All right. Have fun, I guess."

He shut the door and walked down the hallway into the bedroom.

Boy, Carol, how would you have handled something like this? I don't mean Facebook. You handled that beautifully with Alexis. But a girl who doesn't quite know what she's doing on there? I feel like you would have had some kind of sage advice you could pass along to her. Maybe you'd tell her the same thing I told her. Or maybe you would've walked her through it the way Alexis did.

Feeling anxious, he needed to cool off. He walked out of the room and back to the kitchen, where he slipped his shoes on and stepped out into the driveway. The cold air punched him in the face and sent blood rushing through his body. He shivered a little and sighed.

He walked down the driveway to the front of the house and looked at the stars. He heard footsteps, and immediately, he swiveled his head around. *Do they have torches this time? Shoot, the gun's inside. Well, they didn't look that threatening. If I can dodge the sword, maybe I can land a few punches—*

"Evening, Craig."

"Geez!" Craig jumped at the sight of Wendell standing in his driveway. "Sorry, Wendell, I didn't see you there."

"I wanted to ask you about the gunshots from the other night. Did you hear those?"

"Gunshots?" He looked at the sky and tried to feign ignorance. "No, I don't know what you're talking about."

The old man shifted on his feet. "Oh, goodness. Someone used a shotgun over here. I couldn't tell who it was, but I called the cops the second I heard it. I know a shotgun blast from a mile away. They said they couldn't find anyone. I bet it was some idiots walking around on the sidewalk. Maybe they got into a fight or something."

"Yeah, maybe, Wendell. Listen, I should get back—"

"And you know what?" Once he got to talking, he sometimes missed certain cues to end a conversation. "I think it has to do with those guys who tried to break into your house those nights ago. Boy, if I were you, I'd get a security system or something."

Craig nodded politely. "I have it, Wendell. I have my own security system, I guess."

"You can't be too careful in this neighborhood. You never know who's sniffing around. Okay, have a good night." He shuffled away.

You have no idea, Wendell. So you're the one who called the cops this last time, eh?

When his neighbor was a safe distance away, he walked around the house in the snow and looked at the footsteps the Circle had left behind. He laughed as he picked up the chunk of wood that was left from the extinguished torch, dropped by the man who caught the bullet.

I sure wish I had caught more of you with that shot, buddy. And your friends too. Maybe I'll have another chance.

He reached the back yard, the wood still in his hand. Once on the other side of the garage, he looked out over the field, shook his head, and peered at the stars again.

Carol, she thinks of me as a father figure. I guess I'm doing something right there. It sure is hard to feel like a father some days when I don't have the mother by my side. I'm happy she's more comfortable, but that doesn't change the fact that I wish you were here. Even the good times aren't quite as good around here without you.

He hauled his arm back and chucked the wood down the hill into the field before he scanned the area one more time for any movement.

It's as cold as crap out here. I need to get inside and make sure Vickie's not joining a bunch of vampire-related Facebook Groups.

Craig returned to the driveway and jogged back into the house, where he kicked his shoes off. Alexis greeted him as she walked to the sink to fill her glass of water. "What were you doing out there, Dad?"

"Getting some fresh air. How's it going in here?"

She rolled her eyes. "Eh. I think Vickie only wants to use Facebook to talk to Eric. It's not the worst thing in the world, but whatever."

"Great. Now he can stop calling me."

The two of them laughed.

CHAPTER SEVENTEEN

Will and Alexis stood on the walkway that ran along the Milwaukee River and stared at a statue with a gold-orange hue.

The evening was relatively quiet. Not too many people were out and about—exactly the way she had hoped when she'd planned it. *It'll be perfect. No interruptions. He and I can talk about things. And it'll be a peaceful night.*

The river was white, frozen over and covered with a blanket of snow. The sky was clear and quiet. Besides the occasional winter runner, they had the Riverwalk to themselves.

She wore her biggest smile in a last-ditch effort to get Will to show any kind of emotion. For all his smoldering, pretty-boy looks, getting a smile out of him was like pulling teeth.

She threw her arms around the grinning statue with its thumbs jutting outward. "It's hard to believe he was this short, right?"

Will shook his head. "I don't know who this is."

She lowered her arms. “Seriously? The Fonz? You’ve never heard of The Fonz?”

The smiling statue was The Bronze Fonz, a unique little attraction installed on the Riverwalk years before to pay tribute to the *Happy Days* character. Everyone in Milwaukee had, at one time or another, visited The Bronze Fonz and laughed while they took their picture in his iconic *Ayyyyy* pose.

Everyone, of course, except Will. “I don’t get it.”

Alexis sighed. *Movies don’t work. Jokes don’t work. Dances don’t work. He won’t even laugh at silly little stuff like this.* “Will, we have to talk.”

They turned and walked along the river close together so she could stay warm.

“Will, why do you want to be with me?” A lump had already formed in her throat. This was a conversation she did not want to have.

“Because I like you.” His answer was as bland and meaningless as his entire approach to the relationship.

“But why? We don’t have anything in common. You and I don’t gel in any way. I want to have fun and smile and laugh…while you simply sit there with no expression.” The frustration built in her voice. “I like you too. But nothing about this works. I keep trying and I feel like you’re not doing anything in return.”

“Maybe I don’t see any need to try harder. I like things the way they are.” The fact that he could say this with a straight face almost floored her.

“Will, what about this is great?”

“We get to spend time together.”

“Sure, but for what? We don’t do anything. I take you to

places and you don't want to participate in anything. You aren't interested in talking to my friends. You seem more annoyed when you're around them than anything else."

Only when Vickie is around. "I can try harder."

Alexis stopped walking, turned, and rested her arms on the railing as she looked out over the river. She rested her chin on her arms, frustrated into silence. Will stepped forward, leaned over, and put his arm across her shoulders. She closed her eyes and savored the moment because she was reasonably sure it wouldn't happen again.

"This is nice." She said it more politely than romantically.

"Yes, it is. And it doesn't have to stop."

"But it does. I don't know what to do anymore. I don't want to stop this, but I can't be with someone who puts so little effort into a relationship. I haven't seen or met any of your friends or family—"

"I don't have any friends." This almost won the award for Most Unsurprising Statement of the Year.

"Why do you think that is, Will? You don't make any effort to get to know anyone, and you don't let me get to know you either. Like, what is this all for, anyway? I don't get it. I can't keep doing this."

He removed his arm from her shoulders and stared into the distance. "It sounds like you are breaking up with me."

Her lip quivered. "I don't want to. I don't want to break up with you. You're my first boyfriend and I really do like you. I think you're really cute. But I don't know why we're together. I don't know what kind of relationship I'm even breaking up here. Isn't that a problem?"

After a few seconds of silence, Will straightened and extended his hand. "Come with me."

Reluctantly, she obliged. *Is he actually going to open up to me? Was this all I needed to do?*

But Will didn't say a word. He led her down the Riverwalk, then turned into Kilbourn Avenue. Alexis wasn't sure what he was planning to do, but she continued to follow him.

Neither of them wore gloves. She noticed that his hands had grown very sweaty. *What is he so nervous about?*

After a few more minutes of walking, she finally asked. "Where are we going? What's happening? Aren't you going to say anything?"

He turned them both off the street and into an alley. She looked around and tried to think of a reason why they would be there.

Will stepped in close and leaned forward. Alexis didn't know what to do. *He's coming in for a kiss. You're trying to break up with him and he wants to kiss you. Do you simply go with it? Enjoy it while it lasts? You really want to kiss him. Wait—what's that?*

His lips parted and he ran his tongue along his teeth—which had now produced a pair of vicious-looking fangs.

"Will—"

Before she could manage another word, he lunged forward with his mouth wide open. She pushed and shoved but the tips of his fangs pricked the skin on her neck. Alexis screamed in a mixture of fear, disbelief, and pain.

Finally, she punched him as hard as she could on the side of the head. Will took the blow and stumbled back.

She sprinted out of the alley, shouting, "Help!" at the top of her lungs.

Her body trembled as she turned down Milwaukee Street and headed to Cathedral Square Park. She looked over her shoulder and gasped. Will pursued her but he didn't run. Her skin tingled with goosebumps as she watched him slowly and methodically march down the street toward her.

To her relief, she saw a parked police car directly in front of the park. She ran up to it, knocked on the window, and almost scared the officer inside half to death. Crying hysterically, she slapped the window with her hands.

The officer stepped out of the vehicle and held her by the shoulders. "Miss, what's wrong? Are you in danger? Is someone chasing you? What is it?"

Alexis had grown close to incomprehensible in her wailing. She pointed in the direction where Will had been, but he was gone.

She stopped crying in shock and her gaze darted in every direction as she tried to see where he was. "He was there—following me. I know he was. Please, you have to believe me. I'm in danger. I don't know how to stop him."

"It's okay. Stay with me." The officer reassured her with his calm voice. "Let's sit on a park bench here and catch our breath, okay?"

He walked her into the park and helped her to sit on a bench. "Is there someone I can call for you?"

She shook her head and held her cell phone up. With the officer close at hand, she called her dad and asked him to pick her up at the park.

While she waited, Alexis stared at the blue dome of the

steeple of the Cathedral of St. John The Evangelist. *What has happened? Last year, I was a simple girl with a simple life. Now, I live with a vampire while vampire hunters are trying to murder her and I'm dating a vampire? Is this my life now?*

Her father picked her up for a long, quiet ride home. Her silence raised a number of red flags for him.

"Are you okay?"

"I'm fine, Dad."

"Did Will do anything to you?"

He tried to drain my body of blood or turn me into a vampire or whatever, but that's not the answer you're probably looking for. "No, Dad. It was a bad date, that's all."

Her father returned his eyes to the road. "Well, I have to tell you, I don't like this guy at all."

Alexis sighed and rubbed her forehead. "Not now, Dad."

"No, look, I'll say it whenever I want. I have held off on telling you this because I didn't want you to dig in your heels and date him simply to spite me because that's what teenagers do. I don't like Will and I never liked the vibe he gave off—he really bothers me. I don't know what it is, but he bothers me."

She didn't reply. He nodded and decided not to say anything further, satisfied that he had at least told her how he felt.

Back home, she marched into the house and to Vickie's room, where she closed the door behind her.

Her sister was on her bed, typing messages to Eric on Facebook. She looked up with surprise. "Is your date over already?"

Alexis immediately burst into tears and collapsed into a heap on the floor. Vickie typed **I gotta go, ttyl** to Eric and put her arm around the other girl. "What is it? What's wrong? Did Will do something?"

Overwhelmed with grief, she pulled the neck of her shirt down to reveal two bite marks on the side.

The vampire's blood boiled. "Where is he?"

"I don't know," she said weakly. "He disappeared after I found a cop."

"What did your dad say?"

"I didn't tell him."

This made no sense to Vickie. Craig was a protector. "Why not? He would've helped you."

"It could have put him in danger." Alexis blinked a few more tears away. "Sure, he can stand up to the Circle because those are humans. I don't know what happens if he picks a fight with a vampire. And my dad would pick the fight, too. If anyone hurts his little girl—" She burst into tears again.

"Come on, let's sit down. Get your jacket off." She helped her sit on the edge of the bed where she simply stared at the floor. Her sister inspected the bite marks and shook her head.

"I thought vampires didn't bite. I didn't know he was a vampire. I thought you were the last one."

"I am the last one." Vickie stood and crossed her arms. "Will isn't a vampire, he's a Sang. Those are the biters, remember?" Alexis nodded when she remembered the distinction. "I was afraid this might happen."

"Wait, you knew he was a Sang this whole time?" She looked at her, slack-jawed. "I've been out on dates with him by myself, with no way of defending against him, and you knew that he was a Sang? Why didn't you say something to me? Why didn't you try to stop me from dating him?"

"I told you I didn't like him." Vickie knew that answer wasn't enough. "But I thought he liked you. I really did. The only one he seemed to hate was me. I honestly thought you two could still date if he really made you happy. And that's all that mattered to me. I wanted you to be happy."

Alexis rubbed her sore neck. "Well, I'm not happy now." She looked at her sister. "What will you do? Am I in danger now? Will he…hunt me, maybe kill me?"

"Not as long as you're in public. He's like me right now —he can't out himself. Stick with me, and I can defend you in private. But otherwise, stay where he can't hide."

"That explains why he disappeared as soon as I reached the park."

"Exactly. Right now, there is strength in numbers. Let's start there. I'll take care of him beyond that. Don't worry about a thing."

CHAPTER EIGHTEEN

The next day, Craig called the girls to the kitchen table.

Alexis had put on a brave face and deliberately didn't reveal the fact that her relationship with Will had been destroyed and he'd tried to suck her blood. Vickie also played it down and tried to pretend as though she knew nothing and had no intention to kill the boy who hurt her sister.

And while his daughter was definitely on his mind, Craig had other reasons for his request that they sit down with him.

"Girls, we have a problem." He took a deep breath as though he was about to discuss a heavy topic. "You two are getting lazy."

Both girls raised their eyebrows. "Excuse me?" Alexis seemed more offended than the vampire. "Dad, you have to be kidding. We are working hard at school."

He nodded his head. "Yes, and you're both doing fine in school, it seems. I have no problem with that. But outside of school, you don't do anything except go out on dates and hang with your friends—or hole up in that bedroom watching TV or putzing around on Facebook. You need jobs."

Vickie raised her hand. "Aren't we getting paid for the podcast? That's a job, right?" The other girl nodded in agreement.

"Yes, but money isn't the only concern here. I'm talking about work." He winced as he said it, knowing this was tough for them to accept. He didn't want them out of the house all the time, but he knew they were reaching the age when it was time to roll up their sleeves and start working.

"Ugh, I knew this day would come." His daughter hung her head in disappointment. "The days of fun are over forever, aren't they?"

He laughed out loud at the sentiment. "Come on, now. I'm not saying you can't have fun. But even working a few hours a week will get you into the workforce, get you some good experience you can then use on your resume later, and it looks good on college applications. Plus, you make extra spending money to boot. What's not to like?"

"How about the work part of it?" Alexis scoffed. "Come on, Dad, things have been fine. We're responsible."

"I know that, but it's time. My father did the same thing for me when I was your age. I didn't even apply to my first one—he went out and got the position for me. That's how adamant he was about me getting a job."

Vickie folded her hands on the table. "Where will we actually work?"

"That's up to you. There are many places that hire young people at entry level jobs. All you have to do is go out and find one. I'll let you choose what you want." He turned to Alexis. "And because I know you, I have to say this—loosen your standards."

"What?" She looked around in confusion. "Why do you say that to me?"

"It's simple. You are something of a snob when it comes to this kind of stuff. You think you shouldn't do a certain kind of job because you won't like it. Let me tell you something—you're better off going out and doing a job that everyone else is doing."

"What do you mean?"

He leaned forward. Story time. "Back when I was a teen, I decided I wouldn't work in a grocery store like my brother, or in food service like a waiter. I simply wasn't interested in those kinds of jobs."

"What job did you get?" Vickie asked. She was genuinely interested in what this new experience would be like.

"I was an office gofer for a health insurance company."

Vickie drew her eyebrows together. "What does that mean?"

He smiled. "A gofer is merely the office grunt. He's the guy who does all the odd jobs around the office. Some days, I would spend hours filing papers away. Other days, I sat in the back of the office running paperwork through the shredder. That one I did more often than any of the other jobs. They called me Shredder Boy."

Alexis laughed. "That's kinda funny."

"Sure it was. And I was thankful for the job. But here's the thing. I was the youngest person in the office by about twenty-five years. Everyone was older than me, and most of them were women. So I was a kid working around a bunch of older ladies I had nothing in common with. It was a boring job. It paid fine and it was good experience in some respects. But man, it was horrifyingly dull. Day in and day out, I showed up and did my job, but I made zero friends."

"Did you get a different job, then?" His daughter sniffed, apparently not impressed.

"Sure. After that, I took a job as a bank teller."

Vickie's ears perked up. *Hey, I'm a bank teller in my general business class.*

"And after that, I worked as a waiter."

Alexis tilted her head, her expression almost accusatory. "I thought you said you wouldn't work in food service."

Her father nodded sadly. "I did say that. But it doesn't mean I didn't work in food service. I took the job, did well for a couple of years, then moved on. I went wherever the money was good. That's why I waited tables and it's why I was a cashier at a grocery store for a little over a year, too."

"You've had all kinds of jobs, it sounds like." The vampire shook her head. "Why did you have so many jobs?"

He shrugged. "Because when you're a teen, you only look for money, experience, or whatever. You go where the work is. I've been all over the place, and I've had jobs I hated, jobs I loved, and everything in between. In the end, it's all about making money for myself."

Alexis leaned back and crossed her legs. "But Dad, we're doing well, right? The podcast is going well. You're making money. Everyone's fine here. Why are we screwing that up?"

Craig folded his hands and sighed. "I'm clamping down on our budget. I don't want that much pressure on our finances. I'd rather we work hard and save money."

"We can save money any time. Why now?"

His tone became a little more serious. "I don't want to sound like this, but I have to. Alexis, your mother's cancer was devastating to us. It wasn't only a problem emotionally —it was a problem financially. Logistically. Mentally. There was considerable pressure heaped on us that had never been there before. It wasn't something that we could easily manage. It changed how we operated."

"I know that, Dad." She had struggled with the shuffled schedules and the daily way of life that occurred when her mother was diagnosed. "But we made it through that."

"Right, but we barely made it through that. As a family, we went through so much extra stress that we didn't have to deal with—or shouldn't have had had to deal with, anyway. Had we been better prepared, it could have been a much easier transition in many ways. And more importantly, we could have spent more time enjoying Mom's company instead of worrying about how to get things done and pay for stuff."

"You're saying we have to get jobs because one of us might get cancer someday?" Alexis still wrestled to pull the points together.

"Not exactly. What I mean is, life can change on a dime. Even on the smallest basis. Advertisers can change terms with me at the end of our contracts. They can pull money away from us. We can lose massive portions of our income overnight."

Vickie curled her lip. She didn't like that idea.

"And that's only money, girls. One of us could get sick. Something could happen to Vickie. We could all get into a car accident. The house could burn down. I could rattle off a dozen things that could happen to us as a family."

"You're kinda being glass half empty there, Dad." His daughter smirked. She always tried to keep conversations light whenever she could.

"I know. We have to do our best to enjoy life now but also be prepared for what life throws at us. And yeah, that means getting jobs. I'm sorry in advance, but it's something we need to work on if we want to manage life in the future." Neither girl responded. They had given up. "Now, retreat to your rooms and start thinking about job opportunities. Let me know if you have any questions. I'll be in the living room."

The girls did retreat to Alexis's room with their laptops and together, sifted through their different options.

"I don't even know where to start." Vickie shook her head, overwhelmed with the choices. "There are so many things we could do, but I don't know what would be best."

"Did you work at all back in your old home?" Alexis sprawled on her bed, her hands folded behind her head.

"We did work around the house. Most families then were self-sufficient. We grew our own food, made our own clothes, that sort of thing. When you were old enough to walk, you were old enough to work."

The other girl recoiled in disgust. "That sounds terrible."

She shrugged. "It wasn't too bad. It was all I knew. You got up in the morning and you had animals to take care of, a property to manage, and clothes to wash. And, of course, there was always something to clean. It was simply a part of life. Truthfully, I kinda miss it."

"Why?" *Who would possibly miss having to work all the time?*

"It gave my day purpose. Face it, there are days around here where there is absolutely nothing for us to do but watch TV and send messages on Facebook."

Alexis sighed. "Isn't it great?"

"Not really." The vampire laughed at her reaction. "It stinks. I think we are all built to get work done—to achieve something. That's why I am okay with getting a job. Besides, I'd be able to buy more cool stuff. Maybe I'll go back and get that drone thing from the store."

Her sister rubbed her forehead. "That's not why we're getting jobs. If we work and simply spend all the money at once, my dad won't be any happier. We're supposed to save some of the money and use it for important things."

Vickie nodded. "What kind of job do you want to get?"

"I'll tell you what I don't want to get." She sat up and flipped her computer open. "I don't want to work in food service."

"You sound like your dad."

"Right. I don't want anything to do with it. And I'll stick to it, unlike him. There are countless other jobs available where I don't have to carry a tray of food around and serve people. Forget that. What about you?"

Vickie raised her eyebrows. "Oh. I don't know. I guess I wouldn't want to work at that old lady office your dad told us about. That sounds very boring. But other than that? I think I'm open to anything. As long as it pays decently and offers me something interesting to do—that's all I care about."

The two of them searched online for different types of jobs. For a moment, Alexis considered working as a receptionist for a photography studio but decided that would be too boring.

Vickie was overwhelmed with all her choices. "Man, I could do anything. I could wait tables, cook food, bag groceries…where do I start?"

"I knew turning fifteen would be a big year, but I honestly didn't expect this. I thought it would change in fun ways," the other girl grumbled. "Apparently, that's when you start growing up. It was a good ride while it lasted."

Her father heard them discussing it as he walked past the bedroom door. *She's not the only one who has a hard time with this. My little girl keeps growing up.*

CHAPTER NINETEEN

"I don't want to go." Alexis still retained a little depression over Will's unexpected attack. "I don't want to see him or be anywhere near him. I don't want anyone to ask about him. Nothing. I wish I could fake being sick and stay home."

Vickie shook her head and put her arm around her. "I don't think you have to worry about that today. He probably won't come anywhere near you. He won't want to attract attention to himself, so he'll simply stay away. Me, on the other hand? I will make sure I find him."

"What do you plan to do?" Her sister feared any kind of physical violence between the two of them.

"Don't worry about it. You go about your day, try to act normally, and get through it. I'll take care of Will." It sounded like a threat, and it very definitely was. The waiting had only increased her determination.

As the vampire had predicted, Will was nowhere to be seen all day long. Alexis assumed it meant he was home sick—or skipping school. At first, Vickie thought the same thing, and she was disappointed.

But before she stepped into her math class, she paused at the bubbler to grab a drink of water. She'd no sooner leaned over to drink when she felt the now familiar twisting in her gut.

Her thirst forgotten, she straightened and looked around to scan the immediate area. *He's here somewhere. I can feel it. He didn't skip. He's simply hiding. The coward.*

It infuriated her that she couldn't locate him, but she didn't have the time to search in earnest. She continued to attend each of her classes and did her best to concentrate, much like she had told Alexis to do. But after each one, when she stepped out into the hallway, she felt his presence.

After school, Alexis met up with her at her locker. "Are you ready to go home?"

The vampire shoved her books into her locker and slammed the door shut. "No. I'm not. I plan to stick around here."

"Why?"

"Just…go home. Tell your dad I'll catch a ride shortly. I have a meeting I have to attend."

Her sister frowned and tried to recall what she'd missed. "What meeting? I've never heard about you having any meeting." Vickie didn't respond, but the look in her eyes told Alexis exactly what she was doing. "Oh no."

"Just go. Please."

"Don't get yourself hurt." She began to feel overwhelmed with guilt. "This doesn't have to be your fight."

Her smirk said it very definitely was and that she'd made it so. "You have no idea. I'll see you at home."

The other girl patted her on the shoulder and reluctantly left her in the hallway. After about fifteen minutes or so, the school was almost empty. Normally, there were half a dozen afterschool activities practiced or rehearsed during this time but because there was such a heavy snowfall in progress, they were all canceled.

When the building was sufficiently empty, the vampire began to stalk down the hallway and listened to her gut to tell her if she moved closer to him or not. She walked down the English Hall, but the sensation of his presence nearby only triggered when she reached the end of the hall itself.

She marched past the library, the Choir Hall, the auditorium…nothing tripped her senses dramatically, but the faint awareness of him lingered.

When she reached the Band Hall tucked away in the corner of the lower level of the building, it spiked. *He's still here. Somewhere.* She peeked through the windows on the band room doors, but all she saw were darkened instruments. Sure of her instincts, she walked around the hallway surrounding the class, but there was no sign of anyone.

Finally, she opened the back door that led to a lower portion of the parking lot. Will stood alone in the falling snow. He faced her with the cold, expressionless stare that seemed to define him.

Vickie stepped outside, cracked her knuckles, and returned his stare.

"I've been waiting for you." He stretched his neck from side to side as if preparing for something.

"You hurt my friend. This won't end well for you."

"I am trying to survive. Alexis was there. It was nothing personal. I—" Before he could complete his excuses, Vickie lunged at him with full super-speed. She pounded him with her shoulder, and he catapulted into the brick wall on the other side of the parking lot.

He dropped but jumped lightly to his feet, straightened without apparent discomfort, and laughed. "Are we going to play?"

"Make jokes all you want. But you tried to kill my best friend. That means I will kill you." Vickie felt her strength soar as the energy pulsed through her veins.

Will laughed derisively. "Aren't you afraid someone will see us out here? I'd hate for us to be outed like that."

In response, the vampire drew on her super-speed once again and hurtled into another attack. This time, she stopped before the point of collision. Instead, she slid her arm around his neck, twisted, and flipped his body over hers until he sprawled awkwardly in a headlock. He grunted in pain while she tightened her grasp.

"The way I see it, you have no family, no friends, and no one waiting around for you. I could rip your head clear off your shoulders right now and walk away. No one would be any the wiser. No one would know the difference. You'd disappear, exactly like you did hundreds of years ago."

"Like you, right?" Will twisted suddenly, flipped her in much the same way she had done to him, and threw her down before he heaved himself to his feet. "That's the thing about us vampires, Vickie—in today's world, there's not much of a place for us." He leapt toward her with both feet foremost to deliver a kick that drove her through the freshly-fallen snow. The cold, powdery dampness dragged painfully against her face.

She pushed up onto all fours and noticed a trickle of red in the snow. When she patted her forehead with her hand, it came away bloody. "That wasn't very gentlemanlike."

"You threw the first strike. I'm merely retaliating at this point."

Vickie stood and faced him. "Oh, and don't call yourself a vampire. You're not a vampire, you're a Sang. We vampires don't bite."

He shrugged. "Ask anyone in today's world whether or not vampires bite and suck blood. As far as this society is concerned, we might as well be twins." Will barreled toward her using his super-speed, lowered his shoulder, and tackled with enough force that the impact of her landing thrust the breath from her lungs.

As she gasped for air, he crawled on top of her and ran his fingers along her neck. "You know, I've never bitten a vampire before. I was always raised to choose humans. But for you, I might make an exception." He smiled and his fangs protruded from behind his lips.

The vampire raised her knees and shoved him over her head and into the snow. He stood, laughing, as she scrambled to her feet. They were both soaking wet from rolling in the snow, and she was still bleeding from the forehead.

"Ever since I saw you, I've wanted to do this." Will smiled devilishly. "This is fun. It's about time."

"You're sick." She raised her fists in a fighting position.

"I don't know what it is about Sangs that make you so sadistic, but I'm ready to go toe-to-toe with you. Enough of this tackling and shoving business. Come fight me."

"Oh, my dear, I would never hit a girl."

"I'm not a girl, Will. I'm a vampire."

Apparently eager to accept the invitation, he crossed the distance between them and powered a punch at her head. She ducked under it and delivered a crushing uppercut to his jaw. The blow had him airborne for a moment, but he was able to land on his feet. He stumbled, held his face, and laughed once again.

"Nice shot."

"Why did you target Alexis? What purpose did that serve?" Vickie had been consumed by this question ever since they first met.

"Alexis was the closest one to you. I knew you were here and I had to get to you. But I couldn't simply walk up and start doing this." Will attacked in a flurry of fists and both hammered painfully into her stomach.

Again, the wind rushed out of her lungs and she fell, gasping. He laughed as he stood over her. "Like I told you, Vickie, you're my mortal enemy. I was drawn here. I had to be here, and I had to get to you. It's honestly no more complicated than that. I quickly deduced that Alexis was the closest human to you. I needed sustenance, so I thought I would bide my time. I could kill two birds with one stone."

From her prone position, the vampire kicked Will's legs out from under him. He fell hard and the back of his head struck the concrete where the snow hadn't fallen as heavily. She forced herself to her feet and put her shoe on his throat to pin him down. "How did you stay alive this whole time, then? You've been here for months."

As he held her by the ankle in an effort to reduce the pressure on his throat and catch his breath, he smiled again. "You'd be surprised how easy it is to find victims whom no one notices are missing."

Vickie winced in disgust. *He's been killing people this whole time.* "I can't let you live. This has to end now."

She stepped onto his throat and raised her other foot, ready to deliver a decisive blow to his face, but headlights shined onto the snow in the parking lot. *I thought we were alone. Shoot!*

With no other choice, she stepped off Will and darted behind a nearby dumpster for cover. The car rolled through and the driver apparently didn't notice anything out of the ordinary. By the time the vehicle had passed and returned to the scene, her adversary was gone.

"You coward!" she shouted into the silent evening. *Doggone it! You had him. You had him, and you let him go.*

Dejected, the vampire walked up the parking lot to the sidewalk. Thanks to all the snow, there were few people outside walking around. Once she was sure no one would see her, she tapped into her super-speed and ran home in a few seconds.

When she stopped in the driveway, the slippery snow buildup caused her to skid down to the garage door, and she careened into it with a loud bang.

Inside the house, Alexis and her father looked at each other, then jogged to the patio door to see her stand and shake her head vigorously. A bloody splatter marred the white of the metal.

They both hurried out into the snow to help her inside. Once they were in the kitchen, they sat her at the table while Craig inspected the wound. "Are you okay? How do you feel? That was quite a header you took into the garage door."

Vickie shook it off. "I'm okay. That's not from the garage."

Alexis's stomach sank. "Is it from Will?"

Her father looked at her, then back at Vickie. "Did Will do this to you?" She nodded, and his anger burned inside him. "I will go kill him."

"No, you won't. You can't. If you find Will somehow and attack him, you'll simply wind up dead. Alexis can't lose another parent right now."

He looked at his daughter, who nodded. "She's right."

"What's going on? I can't have Will beating you up and not do anything about it."

The girls explained to him what Will was as he cleaned the wound. The vampire then healed herself and closed the gash while he wiped the blood gently from her skin.

Once she was sufficiently tended to, Craig sat at the table and put his face in his hands. *I knew taking in a vampire would bring all kinds of drama, but I have put my daughter in a whole world of danger. How many times did the two of them go out alone? The things that could have happened don't bear thinking about.*

CHAPTER TWENTY

The SUV pulled up in front of Johnny V's. Craig turned and looked at his daughter with concern. "Are you sure you'll be okay?"

"I'll be fine, Dad. Don't worry." She patted him reassuringly on the arm.

"What about Will? What if he shows up and tries to attack you?" He couldn't shake the idea that a frighteningly real supernatural being had attempted to hurt his only daughter.

"First of all, I won't let fear stop me from living my life. Second, Vickie told me Will doesn't want to be outed, exactly like her. As long as I'm in public with my friends, I'm safe."

He took a deep breath, leaned over, and gave her a kiss on the cheek. "Please be safe. Call me if you need anything at all."

"I will. Now, get home and keep an eye on Vickie." She got out of the car and slammed the door behind her.

Craig took another deep breath and tried to keep his

heart rate under control. *She won't let fear stop her from living her life. Do you hear that, Carol? That sounds exactly like something you would say. I think you did say that to me after you were diagnosed, actually. It's amazing how much of you is in that girl.*

He smiled as he put the car in drive and headed back to the house where Vickie was resting. They had all decided to let her have time at home instead of going out with the girls that night.

Inside the diner, Alexis tried to put on a brave face as she greeted Jess and Jamie at their usual booth. After she'd ordered a chocolate shake, Jess leaned over and looked at her friend. "Are you okay? You seem preoccupied with something."

She really had no desire to discuss the trials and tribulations of dating a Sanguinarian who tried to kill her, so she had to think on her feet. Fortunately, there were other things that could reasonably bother her.

"I think I'm simply worried about Vickie."

The other girls nodded in understanding, knowing the girl had more than a few quirks that would concern a friend.

"You know, her school hours are different from ours, so she's kinda on her own this semester." Alexis thanked the waitress when she brought her shake and set it down on the table. "Like…I know she's fine. She's a strong girl."

"Of course." Jamie smiled. "And it's good for her, you know? She needs to be able to make friends and survive without our help all the time."

She pulled the glass toward her and stirred the beverage with the straw sticking out of the whipped cream on top. "Yeah, but I wonder if she's making the right friends."

"Who's she hanging out with now?" Jess took a sip of her Pepsi.

"Apparently, Tricia Rosenberg." She raised her eyebrows in anticipation of the reaction. Both girls groaned.

"Well, I guess she'll have to learn that Tricia isn't exactly a good influence." Jamie folded her arms and rested them on the table in front of her. "But I hope she learns that before she gets too close to her. I can talk to her at lunch about it."

"Try to plant the seed, at least. I don't know if Vickie would rebel against it if someone told her flat-out to not hang out with someone." She wondered if the girl would act like a normal teenage girl when told what to do. "The last thing I want is for her to dig her heels in."

The waitress returned, and the girls ordered their burgers.

"Tricia Rosenberg." Jess shook her head. "I would never have guessed. Tricia is, like, the girl you wonder how she's even in our class. I wouldn't be surprised to see her held back to eighth grade. I don't know that I've ever seen her turn in an assignment on time, and I had several classes with her before she went to remedial."

Jamie giggled. "You know the first time I had a bad feeling about Tricia? Homecoming, freshman year. We were all surrounded by people our age, dancing, and it was totally awkward because we didn't know what we were doing yet. Then I saw Tricia dancing with someone—I would assume her date—and I was like, 'Whoa. That girl has been dancing for a while.'" The girls laughed. "Seriously! She danced all up on him like they were... Honestly, I don't know. But it was gross. That was one of those eye-opening moments."

Alexis sighed. "All I can do is try to be a good influence on Vickie, I guess. Do my best to guide her around whatever phase this is and hope she doesn't get too attached to her. I don't want to pick her friends for her but come on. Tricia is not great."

Soon, the burgers arrived, and the girls paused their conversation to start eating. After a few bites, she wanted to break the silence. Even though she was in public and safe in theory, she still instinctively studied the area in an effort to see if Will was around and perhaps watching her. "Where's Eric tonight?"

Jess nodded. "He heard Vickie wasn't feeling well, so he stayed home to keep her company—messaging her, you know?"

"Awww." Jamie smiled. "That's sweet of him."

Alexis pointed to Jamie. "You know, Vickie is awfully jealous of you."

Visibly surprised, Jamie put her hand on her chest. "Me? For what?"

"She thinks you and Eric have a history, so she's worried he'll leave her for you." She and Jess had a laugh over the idea.

"Oh, my goodness, stop it." The girl couldn't believe the idea that Vickie would be worried about her.

But Alexis insisted. "I'm telling you, it's true. And come on, it makes sense, right? Eric has always liked you. You two are really friendly with each other."

Jamie waved her burger around as she talked. "But we're friends. That's why. And the Eric liking me thing? Just…no."

"Put yourself in her shoes. She's a new girl, probably a little insecure, has a boyfriend for the first time, and hears he's been pining for another girl for a couple of years now —a girl who hangs out with him all the time." Alexis shrugged. "It's not crazy for her to be a little jealous of that."

Her friend pursed her lips and shook her head. "I still think it's silly. Who told her about that?"

"Megan Fitz." Jess nodded in disappointment. "That girl really has it in for her."

"Tell me about it." Alexis lifted her shake and paused before she took a sip. "If I could change one thing, I would get Megan Fitz as far away from Vickie as humanly possible." *Of course, I'd actually want to get Will as far away from me and Vickie as I possibly could. But whatever. I can't say that to them.*

"I know Tricia's a bad influence and all, but I feel like Megan continually brings out the worst in Vickie." Jess dragged a French fry through her cup of ranch dressing. "Whenever you turn around, there she is, stirring the pot."

"You'd think at some point, Vickie would figure that out and simply ignore her." Jamie slapped her thigh. "It's so dumb."

"Yeah." Alexis grimaced, her own history with the girl still reasonably fresh in her mind. "But you know Megan. She knows what buttons to push and how to push them. From what I can tell, Vickie does try to ignore her, but she deliberately crosses paths with her. And every time they wind up together somewhere, Megan has a new way to poke at her."

Jess laughed. "What makes me laugh is that she keeps trying, but in the end, she's the one who ends up embarrassed. Vickie's not the only one who should know better by now."

"Hey, Alexis, so—changing the subject—how are things going with Will? You haven't talked about him in a while." Jamie loved hearing about Will, even though they all knew he wasn't the right fit for her friend. She wanted things to go well because it was nice to see her excited about a boy.

She looked at her plate and deliberately avoided eye contact. "Yeah, that's over."

Both girls dropped their food and looked at each other. "Seriously?" Jess grabbed her arm. "Are you okay? What happened?"

What happened? Oh, he only tried to drain all the blood from my neck. I can look past a few things, but attempted murder isn't really one of them. "It...uh, didn't work out, you know? We went down to the Riverwalk last weekend and talked about it. I told him I was frustrated because he didn't really participate in the relationship. He made no effort to have a good time or even seem like he was enjoying himself. At some point, I had to give up on the idea, right?"

Her friends nodded. They both knew what she was talking about since they had noticed it themselves. "We were waiting for you to see that." Jamie nodded, picked a fry up, and popped it in her mouth. "But we liked seeing you happy. Deep down, though, we had a feeling it wouldn't last very long."

"How'd he take it when you told him all that?" Jess leaned over and took another sip of her Pepsi.

Alexis pursed her lips. *Not too well, I'd say.* "He…didn't like hearing that. But it was the truth. There was no turning back. It had to be over."

"Are you okay?" Jamie leaned in, ever the caretaker of the group.

"I think so. I'm still really bummed out, but Vickie has been a big help. She's stood up for me and when Will needs to be dealt with, she steps in. She's been great."

As the night wore on, Alexis continued to check her surroundings, half-afraid that Will would appear. Finally, Jess noticed that she wouldn't stop looking around. "Are you worried about something?"

She stopped her furtive glances and turned to Jess. "What? No. I just…you know how you have a falling out with someone and you wind up seeing them everywhere?"

"Are you worried you'll see Will?"

"Yeah. I don't think I will, though. He's been hiding out since we broke up. But I do worry about running into him."

Jamie straightened in her chair. "You know, it's weird. I haven't seen him around school all week. I usually see him in the halls at some point. I used to try to wave to him whenever I saw him, but he rarely waved back."

No surprise there. "Yeah, he didn't take the breakup well. I think he's trying to avoid all of us while he…deals with it, I guess." *Or he has decided that since his intended victim is no longer cooperating there's no point in coming to school.*

"Well, we're glad to see you're on the mend and doing okay." Jess raised her glass as a toast. "Here's to a new beginning again. There are many fish in the sea, and more than enough time to find the right one to reel in."

Alexis laughed. *She sure has a way with words. I'm really lucky to have such good friends. Here I am with two girls who take care of me emotionally. Back at home, I have another girl who has protected me physically. For all the twists and turns that life has thrown my way lately, something is really going right here.*

They finished their meal and stood to leave. Her friends both threw their arms around Alexis in a group hug outside the diner while they waited for their rides.

"You're never alone around here, Alexis." Jamie patted her on the back. "You'll always have your friends to watch out for you."

"That's right. And don't you forget it." Jess poked her in the chest. "Lean on us when you need it. And when you're going through a tough time, don't hide it from us. We always find out eventually."

Yeah, well, there are some things I'd rather you never find out, girls.

CHAPTER TWENTY-ONE

Craig opened the door to see Eric standing cautiously on the front step. "Hi, Mr. Watson."

He smiled at him. After hearing about Will, the boy was suddenly far less threatening. "Come on in, Eric."

Relieved, he stepped into the house. "Shame about the Pack this year, huh?" He was referring to the team's collapse in the playoff game the previous week.

The man put his hands on his hips. "Yeah, well, you get used to it after a while. They'll come back stronger next year. Good coaching, a Hall of Fame quarterback…it's only a matter of time until we win another ring."

Eric smiled at him and nodded. *Wow, he's being a lot nicer to me. Maybe Vickie's planning on breaking up with me and that's why he's being nice. Yep, the other shoe is going to drop any minute now.*

"Vickie's in her room resting right now. She knows you were coming, I assume?"

He nodded. "She told me she was home sick. I thought I would come by and check in."

It's nice to see a guy caring about one of my girls. "Go on in."

The boy glanced down the hallway. "Are you sure?" The house had a standing rule of no boys allowed in the bedrooms.

His host gave him a sympathetic look and placed his hand on his shoulder. "This is one time when it's okay. Trust me, I'm not worried about you trying to pull anything in there, not while she's this tired."

Eric smiled again and walked down the hall and into Vickie's room, then shut the door behind him.

Craig, meanwhile, retreated to the living room and put his feet up with a bag of cheese curds on his lap. Vickie had been in bed for a few days by this point. According to her, a fight with a Sang was very different than an altercation with a human. It sapped her of her strength and left her struggling to maintain any energy. Physically—as in wounds or injuries—she was fine, but mentally and in terms of her powers, she was drained.

Inside the bedroom, Eric knelt on the floor beside the bed and brushed her cheek with his fingers. "Hey."

She opened her eyes weakly and smiled at him. "Hey back. It's good to see you."

"Are you okay? You've been down and out for a while, and Alexis hasn't really given me any details. What happened?"

Vickie cleared her throat and blinked a few times as she rehearsed the story the family had come up with. "I have mono."

"Yikes. So no kissing then." He shifted on his knees and

sat back on his heels to create a little distance between them.

She giggled. "No kissing. Not this time, anyway."

He took her hand. "Well, I'm glad your spirits are up. I've really missed you at school. It's funny how hard it is to be away from you when I'm used to seeing you almost every day."

The vampire pushed herself up into a seated position and propped a pillow behind her. The room tilted slightly with the quick moment, and she leaned back until it settled. "No kidding. It really sucks to be laid up like this. But it's a chance to rest and get away from school. Honestly, it's hard to argue with that."

"When will you be better?"

She sighed. "Probably another day or two, I would guess. This isn't really something I've dealt with before, so I'm not entirely sure. But based on how I've been feeling and how I feel now, I'd say a day or two."

"How do you feel now?"

"Like I was run over by a truck." They both laughed. "I'm very tired. But that's okay. I have my TV here to keep me company, and I can always use my laptop and say hi to everyone." She patted the closed device on the bed next to her. "What's happening at school? What am I missing?"

"Not a whole lot." He shrugged and shook his head. "We're all keeping tabs on Alexis to make sure she's doing okay since she's been so heartbroken."

"Good. She needs that. I wish I could be there to help her, too."

"Yeah. And Jamie's really sad that you haven't been around. She says lunch is boring without you there."

Jamie. It always comes back to Jamie. "Listen, I need to ask you a question, and I need you to be completely honest with me."

"Of course."

"Did you ever like Jamie?"

Eric released her hand and used his fists to push himself up off the floor and sit so he could face her. "What do you mean? Like, *like her* like her?"

"You know what I mean."

"What brought this on?" He tried to avoid the question as best he could while he wracked his brain to come up with an acceptable answer.

But he asked a question Vickie didn't want to answer either. She knew how he would react, but she also didn't want to lie to him. "So, Megan Fitz—"

Eric put a hand up. "Megan Fitz? Seriously? Megan told you I had a thing for Jamie and you believed her? Come on, she is only trying to get under your skin."

She gave him a knowing look. "That may be true, but I confirmed it with Alexis. I know you have liked Jamie for a long time."

The jig is up, boy. She knows. "Okay, fine. Yes. I had a crush on Jamie."

Vickie nodded. She felt herself blush with embarrassment. Although she had known the answer and even expected it, she wasn't quite prepared to hear it out loud. "Why are you with me if you like her?"

He raised his eyebrows. "Because she didn't like me like that. She wanted to be friends with me, and that was it."

In a sinister twist, Megan had actually told her the truth all along. "I'm second place, then." A lump formed in her throat, but she tried to keep it together. "You would rather be with Jamie than me, but because you can't be with her, you settled for me."

Eric leaned forward onto the bed and looked directly into her eyes. "That's not true and you know it."

"Really? Then tell me the truth, because that's how it sounds." She was already exhausted, and this news troubled her even more.

Eric paused for a minute to collect his thoughts. "Yes, I asked out Jamie a few times. And yes, I had a major crush on her for a long time. But she and I have always been friends. Even though we will never date, we'll still remain, friends, because that part of the relationship is important to both of us."

Vickie shook her head. "You didn't really prove me wrong there."

"I'm not done yet. Obviously, if I had asked Jamie out and she said yes, I would be dating her. That much is true. But that's because I liked her long before I met you. It's about timing, that's all."

This did little to comfort her. "If Jamie came to you right now and said, 'Okay, let's be a couple. I like you now,' what would you say to her?"

He didn't miss a beat. "I would tell her I have an awesome girlfriend and she missed her chance. 'Sorry, Jamie. But let's stay friends.'"

She didn't believe him although she really, really wanted to. "I still think you'd rather be with her."

He picked her hand up and squeezed it. "The reason we're together is because I fell for you the second I saw you at the airport. That's when I forgot all about my thing with

Jamie. And that's the truth. I did ask her out a long time ago. She said no and I moved on with my life. What's wrong with that?"

"I...I don't know." Vickie struggled to put her feelings into coherent words. "But I wish I could change that. I like Jamie and I think she's great. But it bothers me that you asked her out at one point."

"You never dated while you were back home in Austria? A cute girl like you?" Slipping that little compliment in was intentional. Eric desperately wanted to soften her up again.

"No, I didn't. That's not how things worked in my family."

He crawled up onto the bed and sat beside her, still holding her hand. "Tell me about it. How did dating work in your family?"

She looked out the window. "There wasn't really any dating, actually. Instead, parents were the ones who matched you up with a suitor."

His jaw dropped. "You had arranged marriages in your family? I didn't know that was a thing in that part of the world."

She nodded. "Yep. I was actually close to being matched up before I...came here, I guess. Once you are fourteen years old, that's when they start looking for your future spouse."

"Sheesh. That seems really young. How do you fall in love with someone who is set up to marry you?" He had never known anyone involved in an arranged marriage before.

"Time. You accept it to honor your parents. Whoever you end up with is who you end up with." She hoped this would help him make more sense of her jealousy. "Coming from that, do you understand now? By this age, in my home life, I would be matched up. There are no concerns of cheating or wandering eyes. And there is no feeling of settling."

"I wouldn't say that." Eric shook his head in disbelief. "It sounds like everyone there is settling. You simply let your parents make the decisions for you and that's it? That is so weird. I couldn't do it."

"It's how it was."

"Well, here is very different. At our age, you're expected to date around a little. You try to date one girl, obviously. If it doesn't work out, move on to the next one. There's a right person out there for everyone. But that person won't fall into your lap. You have to go find them. That's what dating is for."

Vickie hadn't really heard it explained to her like that, but it made sense. "You don't still have a crush on Jamie?"

He shrugged. "I still think she's cute. And she's a sweet girl, you know that. But right now, my main focus is taking care of you and making you happy. I love what we're doing here, and I don't want it to stop, especially for something I felt long before you were around."

She opened her arms and he fell into them. Her smile crept in as she held him tightly and kissed him on the top of the head. "I'm sorry I was so jealous."

Eric laughed. "Give me a break. You're coming from a culture where apparently, your life is decided for you when you are fourteen years old. I don't blame you. But please, do me a favor."

"What's that?"

"For the love of all that is good and holy in this world, can you stop listening to anything Megan Fitz tells you? It never ends well, and it only causes you more pain and worry. She has it in for you. Ignore everything she says."

"I'll try." Vickie knew he was right. "I don't know why I always fall for that stuff."

"Because she's good at it. Too good. If you have a question, come talk to me about it. Don't let her play with your mind and then let it stew inside you for too long. I'm here because I want to be with you, not Jamie."

That last sentence finally put to rest any concerns she had. She sighed with relief as she held him, closed her eyes, and exhaled a deep sigh of contentment.

One boy problem was solved. There was still another one to address, but she still had to decide what to do about that one.

CHAPTER TWENTY-TWO

The next morning, Vickie emerged from her room, groggy and a little weak, but walked upright.

From where he sat in his recliner, Craig smiled. "Hey, look who's alive." She nodded blearily at him. "How do you feel?"

She smacked her lips and scowled at the taste of her morning breath. "I need a toothbrush. But I feel somewhat functional."

He put the footrest on his recliner down and closed the magazine he was reading. "Do you feel up to going out of the house?" She hesitated, not sure how to respond. "I mean with me. I won't take you to school."

"Oh. Okay, then yeah. I feel like I could go somewhere. I'm kinda going nuts stuck in this house all day."

"I get that. Take your time and get washed up. Eat some breakfast. Let me know when you're ready and I'll take you on a little grown-up adventure. It won't be as exciting as I make it sound, though."

At that point, she thought anything sounded exciting.

"Dad, honestly, if you only took me to the gas station and back, I'd feel like I was on an adventure. I'm so bored."

He laughed. "Good. I'll be here when you're ready to go."

Her mind raced as she showered and dressed. *I wonder if it's somewhere fun. But he did say it wouldn't be exciting. Anything is better than going to school. Maybe I'm going shopping. Ooh, that would be fun.*

She ate a bowl of cereal as quickly as she could. The anticipation was killing her. When she walked into the living room again, he nodded in approval. "There's the vampire girl I remember. It really is nice to see you back to your old self."

Vickie closed her eyes for a moment. "I'm still a little groggy but it's a start. Where are we going?"

"Let's get in the car."

The two of them climbed into the SUV in the driveway, and Craig drove them down the road without saying anything. A few minutes later, they pulled up in front of a small building that looked like a square hugging a corner, with a pointed roof that seemed sharply out of place.

"This is a weird-looking building." Vickie couldn't even begin to imagine why someone would design a building like that.

"Yeah, I'm not sure about it. I think it was built in the '80s. People must have been more experimental back then or something. I don't know. Let's go in."

They left the car and walked past a large green sign that said *NORTH SHORE BANK* in big, block letters. Without hesitation, he guided her through the double doors and into a dark, almost windowless lobby. A row of bank tellers stood on one side behind bulletproof glass, and three tables with pens chained to them and various slips of paper stacked neatly on top of them stood on the other side.

"Why are we at a bank?" She looked at him in confusion.

Craig reached into his jacket pocket and withdrew a check for eight hundred dollars. "Because of this." He handed it to her, and her face lit up.

"Awesome! More money. We're here to get this cashed?" She already began to dream of what she would spend it on. *Maybe I should go back and try that drone thing.*

But those dreams did not last long. "No. We're here to deposit it."

The vampire didn't understand. "But I don't have a bank account."

"Right. We're here to open one for you."

She looked unimpressed. "That's why we're here? That's the adventure we're on? Grocery shopping would have been more exciting."

The comment made him burst into laughter. "That's good. I told you to keep your expectations low. Look, here's the deal. I gave you the money last time, and you immediately went out and bought a giant TV. And that's fine. It was your money. But it's also my job as your new father to teach you how to manage your money appropriately. That means opening a bank account and showing you the importance of saving your money."

"Saving's not as much fun as spending it."

"Yeah, I get that. Everyone knows that." He walked over to one of the tables with the pen chained to it. "But here's the thing. If you want to buy anything big, you'll need money to do it. In about a year, you'll be able to drive, hopefully. If you are driving, you need a car. If you want a car, you need to buy one, because you definitely won't borrow mine and I can't buy you one. That's where saving money comes in. You start saving these checks now and you'll have a sweet bank account that will allow you to have freedom in your decision making later on."

Vickie stared at him, bummed about the new developments. "I wanted to buy a drone. I have more than enough money for that."

Craig closed his eyes and pinched the bridge of his nose. "Let's open this account quickly so we can deposit this before you spend it. You don't need a drone."

"You're right." She nodded. "I need food, clothing, and shelter. You have those covered. The rest are merely wants."

"It's not only about keeping you from buying a drone, Vickie—although right now, it's partially about that. Do you want to go to college? You'll need money. Do you want to have your own place someday? You'll need money. Oh, and since you and Alexis will have jobs soon, you'll both need bank accounts to have your paychecks deposited to. See how this works now?" She turned and looked at the bank tellers, all of whom waited politely to serve them. "Seriously, Vickie, Alexis gave me no trouble at all when I brought her here to sign up for an account. She was excited. We ordered her a Christmas-themed debit card that she can use."

The vampire laughed at that. "You seem insistent, so let's do this."

After about fifteen minutes of paperwork, they walked

out of the bank and back to the car. "See? That was easy. And now, you have a safe place to put your money and let it grow. You'll be surprised at how quickly that account will skyrocket once you start depositing paychecks from your job."

Vickie let out a yawn. "I'm tired."

"Too much excitement already, eh?" Craig laughed. "That's fine. Let's get back to the house. I think you'll go to school tomorrow."

As they drove in silence, she leaned her head against the cold glass of the passenger-side window.

He glanced at her. "Can I ask you a question about Will?"

She lifted her head. "Sure."

"This might sound dumb, but what would have happened to Alexis if he had bit her? Like, really bit her?" She cocked an eyebrow. "Like, it depends on the story, but in vampire lore, sometimes it kills you and sometimes it doesn't. Sometimes, it turns you into a vampire yourself but sometimes, it doesn't. I don't know what the rules are. How close was I to losing my little girl?"

Vickie ran her fingers through her hair and scratched her head. "Let's put it this way—you were closer than you want to be. It's my understanding that Sangs bite because they want the human flesh, not because they're trying to continue their race. My assumption is she would have died."

"Okay." He gritted his teeth. "Thanks for going after the guy. Believe me, I want to take my shotgun and blow his brains out. But I also don't want you to have to suffer like this all the time. Is there a way that you can...I don't know, finish the job on him? Or do you need help? I want Will out of the picture for good, but I also don't want to risk your health."

"I simply get tired, that's all. I'm not done with him yet. Not by a long shot. I will definitely find him again. When I do, I'll make it very clear where I stand and where he needs to stand as well. And as far as finishing the job goes...I'd like to."

He turned the wheel to the left to enter their home street. "Why didn't you? If you had a big fight with him, why didn't you end it—and him—right then and there?"

"We were in the school parking lot so it's not like we were in the most private of places. I wanted to finish him off, but a car came past. That's how he got away."

Craig squirmed in his seat. He didn't like the idea of actually encouraging a teenage girl to kill a peer. Then he reminded himself that his usual rules didn't apply. *You're not talking to a teenager. You're talking to a four-hundred-year-old vampire who plans to fight with what you can logically assume is another four-hundred-year-old supernatural being. And that second one tried to literally kill your daughter. Encourage all the violence you want with this one. He deserves it.*

"What if I shot him?" he asked, perhaps a little too eagerly. "If we can lure him here and blammo—I blow him away. Then we don't have to worry about him bothering Alexis anymore."

Vickie leaned her head against the headrest and turned to him. "You've seen me in action, right?"

He thought of how she'd disabled the burglars with her super-speed and strength. "Yeah, I remember that. Why?"

"Would you mess with me?"

"Ha! Not a chance."

"Okay, then. Sangs have very similar powers. You could try to kill him, but you wouldn't last long. He still has the speed and the strength to neutralize you before you could fire your first shot."

He nodded disappointingly. "That's too bad. Sending you to do it instead is again, to me, option number two."

"What's option number one?"

"Taking my gun and filling that jerk with bullets."

CHAPTER TWENTY-THREE

Another week had passed since Vickie returned to school, and she worked very hard to make up for lost time.

Teachers extended her a little grace, although none of them knew of the "undisclosed medical issue" that kept her at home. Because Alexis had a spotless record and no one suspected any bending of the truth on the part of her father, everyone accepted the excuse without question.

But now that she was back, it was time to focus on the books and work hard. In the mornings before school, she sat shoulder-to-shoulder with Eric and worked on her homework. During lunch, she was pleased to be comfortable around Jamie again, but she still had homework to do. And after school, she returned home and continued with her homework.

All the while, she felt surprisingly comfortable. She didn't sense any threat from the Circle, and Will's presence didn't intrude on her daily routine. Still, both were odd, and she reminded herself that while both parties might have retreated for now, they were equally real and dangerous. It was a thought that niggled constantly at the back of her mind.

At dinner one night, she explained the concern to Alexis and her father, both of whom seemed encouraged by it.

"I think the Circle was scared off when they realized we were armed." Craig pointed at the two of them with his fork as he chewed. "They probably retreated to Austria to hide out. Come on. They came all the way over here to kill you and assumed you wouldn't put up much of a fight as a teenage girl. Plus, since they had that sword, they could keep you weakened anyway. They didn't count on me packing heat."

Alexis laughed while she twisted spaghetti onto her fork. "Dad, you're so lame."

"What's so lame about that?" He was taken aback by the comment. "Look, this house is protected. They didn't know it was protected and now, they must realize it's useless. Maybe I didn't kill any of them, but I sure as heck scared them off."

His daughter nodded in agreement. "You might be right about that. And hey, maybe that's what happened with Will, too." She forced a smile through the small trace of sadness on her face. "You took the fight to him. Maybe it wiped him out worse than it hurt you. I don't know. But I bet he gave up and decided to get out of here before anything else happened to him."

Vickie took a sip of her milk. "I hope you're both right. I don't think you are, but I hope you are."

"Why do you say that?" Craig put his fork down and

folded his hands.

"Because it seems too easy. It suggests that all our loose ends were neatly wrapped up simply because we fought back a little. These are people who claim to be my sworn enemies. They are unlikely to give up that easily."

That night, she assured Eric that she was almost caught up with her work.

Vickie: *Just give me another day or two to finish, then we can hang out, babe. I'm sorry*

Eric: *It's okay! You were out for a long time. Take care of that homework first, I'm not going anywhere ;-)*

The winky-face made her smile. *Such a sweet, supportive guy. I'm really lucky to have him.*

The next day, she still struggled to get through her schoolwork as new assignments piled on top of the old.

When she reached the library, she sat at the table with Tricia, who wondered why she was working so hard.

"I'm running out of time. I have to have this checkbook and budget finished for general business class or Mr. Numerich will have a cow." She opened her folder to produce the papers for the project.

"I thought you did that already." The other craned her neck to see the assignment. It looked exactly like past budget assignments Vickie had done.

"No, you have to keep doing it. Every month, you have to create a new budget and fill out the checkbook with your expenses."

Tricia didn't understand the problem. "So make some stuff up. How hard is that?"

"You can't make it up. It has to be verifiable. I have to

search for the prices and cite my sources." She sighed loudly enough that one of the librarians shushed her.

Her companion leaned in. "Why don't you ask for an extension or something?"

"I did that already. I've had extensions. This is only one of the last assignments I'm catching up on and I'm really wiped out. I've fallen asleep at my desk every night this week."

Tricia leaned over and closed the folder, sat beside her, and pulled the papers out of her hands and tossed them aside.

"What are you doing?"

Her tone was calm and reassuring. "You will go in there and get another extension."

"No, you don't get it—"

She raised her hand. "You've been sick and are overworked, and it's detrimental to your health. You'll go in there and get another extension on the project. All you have to do is talk about how overwhelmed you are, and he will cut you some slack. Meanwhile, you look terrible. You have thirty more minutes left in this period. Put your head down and take a little nap."

Vickie was torn. She wanted to catch up on her work, but a nap did sound tempting. "I don't know."

"I think your teachers would prefer you to be alert and attentive during class, right? Put your head down and nap now while you can, and you'll be as fresh as a daisy for your next class."

Reluctantly, she put her head down on the table. Within two minutes, she was fast asleep. Tricia nodded approvingly and returned to reading a magazine.

When the bell rang, Vickie woke and gathered her things. "Thanks."

Tricia smiled. "What are friends for?"

When the vampire arrived at general business class, however, things were not as simple as she had been assured they would be. She walked into the classroom and set her things down. Slowly, Mr. Numerich walked up the aisle and greeted her quietly at her desk.

"Miss Hewitt."

"Hi, Mr. Numerich."

"Today is the day when your budget is due. I trust you have finished it."

"About that...yeah, I have really struggled to catch up on my work."

He nodded, but she could tell he wasn't buying it. "Working after a long absence can be difficult. That is why I gave you an extension on your deadline. But that extension ended today."

Uh oh. He's pushing back. Shoot, you should've simply done the assignment in the library like you wanted to. "Mr. Numerich, I'm sorry. Only a couple more days and—"

"I am sorry, but you have had more than enough time to catch up on your work. Unfortunately, I will have to give you a zero on this portion of the project, and because it was not turned in, I have to give you detention as well." He spoke calmly and in a very measured tone so as to not draw attention to the exchange in front of the class.

"But...but..." She stammered, completely at a loss as to how to react to any of this.

"That is all. You can pick your detention slip up at the

end of class today." With that, he turned and walked to the front of the class to begin the lesson.

Vickie sagged in her chair. *For all the hard work, the late hours, the constant focus on catching up, I'll still get a zero and detention? But I've tried so hard. Tricia said everything would be fine.*

The vampire couldn't enjoy the class at all. It had become more and more practical as the semester wore on, which had captured her interest. But that day, nothing could revive her enthusiasm.

Mike Arroyo, as he always did, waited for the teacher to face the chalkboard and begin writing before he called loudly, "Bubbles!" in a silly voice. This always produced stifled laughter from the class, including from Vickie.

Bubbles was allegedly Mr. Numerich's name when he worked as a circus clown—an urban legend at Clear Lake High School.

The rest of the class was a blur, and Vickie stopped at his desk at the end of the period to collect her detention slip. For his part, Mr. Numerich looked disappointed.

"I understand it's been tough for you, Vickie. You're a good student. But I can't offer you special treatment at the expense of your schoolwork." He waved his hand to dismiss her, and she shuffled out into the hallway.

After school that afternoon, Alexis met her at her locker and was shocked to hear she had detention. "Already? Geez, you've only been back a few days. What did Megan Fitz do now?"

Vickie threw her books angrily into her locker. "It wasn't Megan. I didn't get my general business homework done in time and Mr. Numerich wouldn't give me another extension. Can you believe that? I'm a good student, and I was dealing with a big delay from being sick. The guy could at least have a little compassion."

Alexis stepped back. "This doesn't sound like you. I thought you planned to get that done today in the library, anyway. You said you were on track to get everything caught up."

She stopped throwing books and leaned up against the bank of lockers. "I was, but I was so stressed out, so Tricia told me to put my head down—"

"Hang on, why would you let Tricia tell you to do that? If you're late with work, you can't simply take a nap." She had been concerned that exactly this kind of thing might happen.

"She said I could get another extension. I wanted another nap. It all made sense at the time." She rested her head on the lockers behind her.

"Vickie, Tricia Rosenberg is a classic manipulator. She works everyone up so they fall for whatever line she throws at them."

"Even teachers?"

"Especially teachers."

Vickie thought she should at least be as convincing as the other girl. "Then how come I wasn't able to get another extension, but Tricia can in her classes?"

Alexis put her hand on the lockers and leaned on it. "Does she have Mr. Numerich for any of her classes?"

"I don't think so."

"No, she doesn't. Tricia is in remedial classes. Her teachers already go easier on her."

"Okay, but that's because she struggles with the work,

right? That's how you get into those remedial classes." She didn't quite understand what her sister was trying to say.

The other girl's tone grew more frustrated. "No, it's not because she's slow. Tricia is not dumb at all. I've talked to her before. She seems bright enough. The reason she's in those classes is because she's lazy. She spends her off time drinking and hanging out with boys and who knows who else. Tricia isn't a good student, that's why. She refuses to apply herself and instead, wants to coast through life."

This didn't match up with Vickie's perception of her. "She seems nice."

"Oh, she seems great now. But she's the reason you will go to detention in a few minutes instead of going home. And you still have general business homework to do tonight. You could have had the night off, but you listened to bad advice instead."

Alexis tried not to get too worked up. The vampire felt like she belonged, but she still had so much to learn about certain types of people. She mustered a little sympathy for her.

"Go to detention. Serve your time and call when you're done. My dad will pick you up. Try to learn from this, okay? Tricia seems nice, but she won't be nice when she doesn't get what she wants. Please be careful about that."

With that, she left her and headed to the door, while the vampire picked her backpack up and wandered disconsolately to the study hall for detention.

As she sat in silence—serving her time, as her sister had called it—she couldn't quite shake the feeling that something bad was about to happen.

Again.

CHAPTER TWENTY-FOUR

There were two types of students who served in detention, as far as Vickie could tell.

First, the regulars. These were the kids who were almost always there, generally for bad behavior or breaking school rules. They brought drugs into school, started fights, were chronically late to class or sometimes, didn't bother to show up at all.

She could easily point out a regular by their overall attitude and demeanor. Some of them slept through the entire thing. Others stared mindlessly off into space. Still others tried to goof off and drew the ire of whoever was in charge of monitoring the session that afternoon.

The other group of students was the one-offs, of which she was a member. They were there due to an unexpected error or minor infraction. These students were not used to being in detention and generally used the time to get homework done. They always appeared uncomfortable to be there and tried to keep their heads down and power through the time allotted.

Normally, she would have done the same thing. She had considerable homework to do, and this would have been a great time to do it.

But on that day, she felt too distracted. Her stomach was in knots. *He's here. I know it. He's somewhere, but he's waiting for me.*

The clock couldn't move fast enough. Vickie wanted out—not so she could get home but so she could find him. She wasn't at full strength, but she didn't need to be.

Don't you dare go anywhere until I get out of here. I want to get my hands on you.

She sneered as she counted the minutes down. Finally, when they were dismissed, she slung her bag over her shoulder and made a beeline for the same tucked-away area in the parking lot where they had confronted each other before.

It's the only place where you can get into it without doing too much noticeable damage to property. I know he's there. He wants to do this as badly as I do.

Aggravated, she shoved the door to the parking lot open and saw Will waiting with a satisfied smile on his face. He calmly removed the long black peacoat he wore and tossed it aside when he saw her burst through the door.

She dropped her bag. "What did you wait so long for?"

He looked down his nose at her. "I wanted a fair fight. We didn't have the chance to finish last time. I knew you'd be tired." As she stepped closer, he tilted his head to study her. "You're still tired. You're not one hundred percent at all."

"I'm strong enough to take care of you, Will. It's funny.

If you had only smiled like that once in a while around Alexis, maybe you'd have gotten closer to her. But you couldn't even pretend to be a human being."

His smile dropped in favor of a look of disdain. "Ugh, why do you want to be a human being anyway? These people are terrible. They deserve what they get."

"You don't feel bad about preying on the weak?"

The question provoked a rare laugh from the Sang. "Natural selection, Victoria. Only the strong survive." He raised his fists.

"And I intend to." She hurtled forward but stopped abruptly in front of him and he flinched instinctively. With only a limited amount of her usual strength available, she knew she had to use it wisely.

Once she'd caught him off-balance, she grasped him by the back of the neck and his arm and powered him into the concrete with such force that a large crack slivered through it.

Before she could capitalize on it, he caught her legs and yanked her down with similar force. She pushed up onto her hands and knees, dazed from the impact.

Will retreated to a safer distance to compose himself. Then, as she rose to her feet, he lowered his shoulder and drove into her. The impetus of their collision catapulted her into the large green dumpster behind her.

The ensuing crash echoed in the evening silence and left a massive dent in the side of the container. From where she lay, Vickie shook her head as she looked at the damage. *Not again. The school will begin to get really curious about this.*

He attacked once again, and she scrambled into a seated position and met him with a forceful punch to his face. The blow hurled him into a somersault that ended in a solid thump when he landed.

Vickie stood and cracked her neck. She took a moment to force her cuts and scrapes to close and used some of her limited energy to do so. Will struggled to his feet and used the time to address his injuries, which immediately healed as well.

"What do you want from me, Will?"

"The same thing you want from me." He spun into another assault. This time, when she tried to punch him, he stopped short and let the momentum of her swing turn her and wrapped his arm around her neck.

She flailed her arms and legs in vain. His hold was far too unyielding for her to fight free. He leaned in and sniffed her. "You may pretend to be a human, but you still smell like a vampire."

Ugh, that's disgusting. She tried to speak, but he had clamped down on her windpipe as tightly as he could.

"Now, you remember, Vickie...what's the only sure way to kill any of us? That's right, beheading." He tightened the pressure around her neck. "I don't happen to have a sword or knife with me, so I'll have to settle for simply ripping your head off your shoulders instead. I hope that's okay."

Her vision started to blur, and her hearing muffled as she began to lose consciousness.

"But hey, just for fun, I'm a little hungry." He loosened his arm on her enough to slip in and sink his fangs deep into her neck.

The vampire groaned in pain through gritted teeth. A mixture of sweat and tears rolled down her cheeks while Will sucked the blood from her body.

Instinctively, she kicked blindly and dislodged his arm enough for her to be able to kick him again. This time, she managed to add a little of her power to shove him a few feet away.

She collapsed but spun quickly to face him so he couldn't sneak up on her. Blood streamed from her neck and into the sewer through the grate she'd landed on.

Vickie looked away from the red trail to where Will sat and laughed with blood all over his chin and down his own neck.

"You sick freak." She coughed. As she reached tentatively to feel the wound, she noticed a chunk of flesh from the side of her neck was missing. If she wanted to heal that, it would take almost all of her energy to do so—and she wouldn't be able to do it again.

She opted to bleed for a few minutes to conserve her energy. "You don't understand."

He dragged himself to his feet. "What don't I understand, sweetheart? You're my mortal enemy. History precedes us. We can't coexist."

"Why not?" She grunted and winced from the pain in her neck. "Those were the old days. This is a new time—we can change the way things work."

He laughed and shook his head. "You're exactly like the rest of the vampire race—a group of peace-loving weaklings who would rather fit in than stand up for themselves. The human race doesn't want you. If they find out about you, they will kill you. You will have survived four hundred years for nothing. Don't you understand that?"

Vickie stood slowly and looked him in the eye. "Do you think that by killing me and being the last Sanguinarian on

Earth, you somehow have a leg up? Look around you, Sang. You know as well as I do that there are no more left. You're the last of your kind and I'm the last vampire. That's it. The human race has won. The best we can do is try to fit in."

"I don't hide." He licked his lips, which elicited nausea in her.

"Yeah, right! You've been hiding this whole time. What happens when you kill me, huh? If you kill me, you simply continue to hide and what? Kidnap people? Kill them in the darkness? Someday, they'll catch you and they'll kill you. It's inevitable. If you continue down this path, you'll be as dead as I would be—unless you fit in."

He closed his eyes. "A fine speech. Really." He curled his lips and bared his fangs as he prepared to feast.

Despite her instinctual surge of fear and revulsion, she wouldn't back down. "Maybe the humans here don't know about us, but that doesn't mean we're hidden. The Circle is here."

Will backed off for a moment. "The Circle?"

Vickie nodded desperately. "The Slayer Circle. They're here. They've tried to attack me several times. They have the sword that murdered my parents, your parents, and all our ancestors. Do you want to kill someone? Well, then, let's kill them. Let's eliminate them from this land so we can figure out how to peacefully coexist. Otherwise, they'll kill me, and I bet they'll kill you too."

He stepped away with his hands on his hips and stared at the ground. "Are you sure they have the sword?"

She nodded. "I held it in my hands."

"What happened?"

"I lost everything. I was nothing but a human being, robbed of all my powers." The vampire felt a little more encouraged. *Maybe I'm getting through to him.*

"Where are they now?"

"I don't know. They haven't shown up for a while, but I'm sure they are merely biding their time. Together, we can fight them. Alone, I'm not sure I can."

They stood in silence for a few seconds before she finally lost her patience. "If you want to kill me, fine. But they'll target you next." She knelt in the parking lot, closed her eyes, and used the last of her energy reserves to heal the gaping wound in her neck.

When it closed, she sat on her heels. Her eyes still closed, she called out. "Now's your chance. I can't continue this fight anymore. Kill me."

After several seconds of silence, she opened her eyes cautiously. Will was gone.

She struggled to her feet and leaned against the dumpster to catch her breath. *I don't know if I convinced him or not, but I won't wait around to find out.* She tried to open the doors to enter the school, but they were locked now that everyone had left.

After another moment to steady herself, she scrabbled in her backpack and retrieved her dirty gym shirt, wiped her neck so the blood wasn't so noticeable. That done, she shuffled out of the parking lot to the gas station on the corner, where she could call Craig and have him pick her up.

CHAPTER TWENTY-FIVE

Craig knew instantly that Vickie had been in another fight with Will.

"What happened? Are you okay? How badly are you hurt?"

She waved him off. "It's okay. Really. I…I'm fine. I'm very tired, but I'm fine."

They drove down the road and he shook his head. "You can't keep doing this, Vickie. Something has to give. Are we supposed to take you out of school now for another week? We can't do that. You're almost caught up. Besides that, it's reached a point where I wonder whether or not you'll be dead every time I pick you up."

The vampire had no answer for him.

"I worry about you, okay? I don't want you to be hurt. We didn't bring you here to be killed. We could've saved considerable hassle by leaving you in Austria if that were the case."

Vickie took measured breaths and fought to keep her

composure. "He could've killed me today. He really could have. I gave him the opportunity."

Craig immediately pulled the SUV to the side of the road and pushed it into park. "Are you kidding me? You gave him the chance to kill you? Why would you do that?"

She looked at her hands clasped in her lap. "I don't know, really. I only… I wanted an end to all this. I tried to make a point and I think part of me knew he wouldn't. That sounds strange to say, I know, but I knew he wouldn't. I gave him an opening and he backed off. I told him it wouldn't accomplish anything—that his anger at me for hiding who I was should be directed at himself. He would have to hide either way and killing me wouldn't change that."

He leaned back in his seat and stared out the windshield. "Having you for a daughter is a rollercoaster of emotions sometimes."

Her smile was a little weak, but she managed it. "I know. And to be honest, like, a third of my neck was missing. I had to use what little energy I had left to heal it, or I would have bled to death anyway. It's not like I was perfectly healthy and gave him a free shot."

He sighed and eased the car back into traffic while he imagined the horror of Alexis having her neck chewed to pieces. *If she hadn't gotten away, that would have been her.* He shuddered. "So what now?"

"I have no clue. I don't know where he went and if he will leave me alone entirely, or what. Maybe he'll come back and finish the job later. I only hope I have the energy to put up a fight."

Craig daydreamed about sharpening knives in preparation for that encounter as they drove home.

Vickie struggled through class for the rest of the week and despite her absolute exhaustion, made sure her homework was turned in on time. Part of the reason she worked hard to get through it was what Craig had told her—it would be really difficult to take her out of school again.

But the other reason was much more selfish. She had a date with Eric for Friday night.

He had let Alexis go out on dates with Will on her own and now, it was Vickie's turn to be entrusted with a little independence. He drove them both to the town of Brookfield and dropped them off in front of a burger joint called Fuddrucker's.

"All right, you two, have a good dinner and have some fun. When you're done, walk to the mall and hang out for a while. I'll pick you up at eight o'clock. Does that sound good?"

"You got it, Uncle Craig."

"Thanks, Mr. Watson."

They climbed out of the car and slammed the door excitedly. Craig watched Vickie bounce on her heels. He was happy to see a little spring in her step again. *That girl has worn herself out so much. She deserves to have a good time tonight. I only hope Will doesn't show up out of nowhere or something stupid.*

They both took deep breaths while they looked up at the Fuddrucker's sign and listened to the car drive away.

"Well, this is it," Vickie announced.

"Our first real, official, all-by-ourselves date." Eric smiled widely and took her by the hand. "Have you ever been here before?" She shook her head. "Oh, you'll totally love it."

They walked through the doors, her senses were immediately assailed with neon lights, kitschy knick-knacks, and obnoxious signage in every direction. "I don't know where to look first."

From the Miller Lite flags bearing the Milwaukee Brewers logo strung across the ceiling to the countless pictures and signs proudly boasting the *Fresh Daily!* beef, to the Wisconsin-themed flags, signs, logos, and tchotchkes, Fuddrucker's was almost overwhelming.

They both stood in line to order their burgers and each settled on a bacon cheeseburger with fries. The cashier handed Eric a number, and he took it along with the two plastic cups for soda and they ventured deeper into the restaurant.

While he walked to the soda dispensers, she paused in front of a section called the Machine Shack. "What's in there?"

"Oh, that looks like an arcade. Video games, that kind of stuff. We can play after we eat. The burgers won't take long."

They found a small two-person table around the corner from the arcade section and settled in. Awkwardly, they exchanged eye contact and giggles as neither really knew how to act.

"This is silly." She shook her head and tapped her hands on the table. "We've been together for a while now. We've been alone before. Why does this feel awkward?"

"Because it's new. We have ultimate freedom for a few hours. We're simply overthinking it." He stared off into space and tried to come up with a topic of conversation. "Hey, have you seen Will around? He's been missing from school for like, weeks."

You could say I've seen him a few times. "No, I haven't. Since he and Alexis broke up, it's like he disappeared off the face of the Earth." *I wish.*

"It's so weird. I know he was a little awkward, but I thought he was a nice guy."

That's because you didn't see his teeth in my neck the other day. "He was okay but wasn't a good fit for Alexis, though."

He shook his head vehemently. "Oh, no way! They were terrible together. I don't know what his type is, but it definitely isn't her."

They laughed as the server brought their burgers. They ate carefully to avoid smearing food on their faces. For Eric, it reminded him of eating spaghetti at Homecoming. *What is it about eating around this girl that makes me so self-conscious? I ate lunch around her for a whole semester with no problems.*

After they ate, they tried out a few games in the Machine Shack as he had promised. Vickie marveled at the graphics on the racing game, and she shared the universal frustration of not being able to snatch a stuffed animal at the claw game.

Once they were done, they huddled together outside the restaurant and crossed the parking lot to the Brookfield Square Mall.

For a few hours, they window shopped and simply drifted from store to store while they discovered what they each liked and disliked. Eric was clearly a big Green Bay

Packers fan and lit up with excitement when they entered a sports memorabilia store.

It was there that he regaled her with the stories of Packers legends and memorable moments.

"This photo here is right before Bart Starr hiked the ball and dove into the line. It was, like, fifteen below zero during the whole game, but these guys went out there and did their thing. He scored a touchdown on this play and sent the Packers to the championship. We call it the Ice Bowl."

"Now, over here, this is Brett Favre—the longest-playing quarterback in Packers history. He played more games in a row than any player. The guy was made of steel."

Vickie pointed to the photo in question. "He looks really happy. But why does he have his helmet off? Shouldn't he wear that if he's on the football field?"

Eric shook his head, chuckling. "No, this was after the play was over. It was the first touchdown he threw in the Super Bowl. He was so excited, he yanked his helmet off and ran around the field like a little kid. Classic moment."

She wandered down the aisle until she saw a familiar face. "Okay, this picture is Aaron Rodgers, right? The quarterback we have now? What's on his shoulder?"

"That is a championship belt. Pro wrestling gives a big gold belt to the best wrestler. It's kind of a thing. When the Packers won the Super Bowl that year, they gave Rodgers a belt to wear."

The vampire wasn't that into football, but she enjoyed seeing Eric all excited about it. She could see him relax and enjoy the date instead of worrying about what he would do next.

They wandered through the entire mall and even stopped to ride a virtual reality rollercoaster that blew Vickie's mind. "I don't understand how any of this works. I really don't."

"I don't either, but isn't it fun?" He threw his arm around her and squeezed her tightly after they climbed off the machine. She took his hand, looked at him, and they shared a kiss.

After they both blushed, they stopped for gelato and shared a cup of chocolate before they resumed their stroll.

The announcement over the PA system intruded into their relaxed pleasure. "Attention, Brookfield Square visitors. The time is now eight fifty-five pm. The mall will close in five minutes. Please finish your transactions and make your way to the exits. Thank you."

They looked at one another in total panic. "It's almost nine?" Eric's stomach sank. "Your uncle will be furious."

The duo sprinted through the mall until they saw Craig power-walking in and out of every store in search of them. When he saw them, his face was beet red. "Where have the two of you been? I've waited here for an hour!"

"It's all my fault, sir." Eric stepped forward and tried to calm him. "I lost track of time. I should have paid closer attention. I should have called or something."

"I'm happy you're okay, but you had me really worried. If you want to go out on dates, you have to be aware of the time."

"You're right. I'm so sorry." Vickie folded her hands in front of her chest. "We honestly didn't do it on purpose. It wasn't only Eric's fault. I should have watched the time as well."

"We had so much fun together, that's all. But that's no excuse." Eric looked like he was about to cry.

Craig sighed, then turned to walk to the car. "Come on, let's go. There's nothing we can do about it now and no sense in getting any more upset about it."

The ride home was very quiet. Eric was terrified to say anything, and she was exhausted, having still not fully recovered yet from the beating sustained at Will's hands.

After an awkward good night at Eric's front door, father and daughter drove back to the house, while he wore a permanent scowl on his face.

CHAPTER TWENTY-SIX

Craig's bad mood didn't last long. After submitting applications and going out on interviews, the girls had both landed their first jobs.

"Dad, don't be lame." Alexis rolled her eyes as her father insisted he take a photo of her standing by the front door before he would take her to work. Vickie sat at the kitchen table and laughed. "Yeah, you just wait. Your turn comes next week. I'll be sure to laugh at you, too."

He dropped her off at the Bradley Road Market, a small grocery store five minutes down the road from their house. She wasn't thrilled with the idea of working in a grocery store, but it ticked off several boxes in her mind. It was open late, so after-school hours were easy to come by, there were many coworkers, so shift switching would presumably be easier, and it was close to home, so it was easy to get to.

She walked through the cramped entrance and past several rows of shopping carts before she reached the main customer service desk.

"Uh, hi. My name is Alexis. It's my first day."

The bubble blonde behind the counter greeted her with a warm smile. "Ahhhhh, new girl. Matt left your ID back here. Hang on, I'll get it." Alexis nodded and turned to observe the rundown, dated-looking grocery store. "Here you go." She handed her a badge that said *ALEXIS* on it. "There's a stripe on the back. Go over there and swipe it in the machine. That's how you punch in and out. I'll call Matt and let him know you're here."

After a couple of failed attempts, she finally got the machine to give her the green light indicating she had successfully clocked in. When she turned, a stout, dark-haired man in a white shirt and black pants emerged from a door behind the bakery.

He extended his hand. "Alexis? I'm Matt. Nice to meet you. Welcome. Follow me and we'll get you a shirt." He was gruff and matter-of-fact, which she didn't mind. "You interviewed with Chris, right? He owns the place."

"Yeah. Tall guy with glasses?"

"That's Chris." She expected some kind of follow-up to that question, but it never came.

They walked through the door behind the bakery, which led to the back area of the store. On the right was a set of bathrooms of questionable cleanliness. Directly ahead was a break room with even more questionable cleanliness. The open area was the stock room, overloaded with pallets of canned goods, processed food, cereal boxes, and laundry detergents.

She followed her guide around a few pallets to a small windowless room tucked away next to the large garage door and a massive red machine. "Wow, what's that thing?"

Matt looked over his shoulder and kept walking. "That's the baler. It's where you put cardboard boxes. You'll get to know it. Until then, don't touch."

He stepped into the small room and reached behind the door to retrieve a fistful of green striped button-up shirts. "What are you—a medium or a small?"

Alexis looked down at her shirt. "A medium is fine."

He tossed her one. "Okay, put that on and tuck it in. We do not work with shirts untucked. If the front doors are opened and your shirt is untucked, you answer to me, got it?"

This had not started out as well as she'd hoped—and she honestly had low expectations going into it. "Got it."

Matt nodded. "You can hang your coat here in the office. The hook is behind the door. Let's go to the break room."

Alexis ducked quickly into the office to hang her coat up, then frantically threw on her new work shirt and tucked it in before she reached the break room.

The term was used loosely, that much was obvious. There was a small computer at a desk to train new hires, two folding tables, and a scattered assortment of metal folding chairs all under a pair of fairly dim light bulbs. There were no vending machines and no TV or radio, merely a place to sit and eat.

"Have a seat." Matt stood at the computer. She obliged and carefully kept her expression neutral. "This is your trainer for today. You'll spend a few hours here, so get comfortable. It'll teach you the basics about store policy, how to use the cash register, and all that fun stuff. After each unit, there is a test. You need ninety percent or better to continue to the next one. Otherwise, you have to retake the entire unit until you pass. After each unit, you can take a five-minute break to stretch your legs and walk around, but don't wander too far. If you take a longer break, trust me, I will know. If you have any questions, I'll be back here. Good luck and welcome to Bradley Road."

She was taken aback by how blunt he was. Until now, she had been so used to schoolteachers who were pleasant to her and made sure she felt welcome. But Matt had clearly worked at the store for a long time and had seen any number of new hires. He didn't pretend to be happy to see anyone and simply did his job.

Well, let's try to make the best of it. This will definitely be boring but look on the bright side. You'll make eight bucks an hour to sit at a computer. It could be far worse.

She was right. The computer lessons were very boring. Much of the job was common sense, and she breezed through each lesson. Her confidence grew. *Maybe I'll turn out to like this job.*

As she thought that, a short, skinny little man with slicked-back greasy hair, a wispy beard, and a permanent scowl on his face shuffled into the break room with a bag of chips and a soda. He pulled his phone out and sat facing her and simply stared at her while he shoveled chips into his mouth.

Alexis turned to look at him and he made no effort to stop. "I'm Andy." He spoke through a mouthful of chips.

"Hi. I'm Alexis." He nodded at her and continued his rudeness unapologetically.

Maybe this job won't be so great.

The following week, Craig put Vickie through the same

torture and took a photo of her at the front door. "First day of work," he announced in a cheesy voice.

Vickie laughed at him, however, before they piled into the car and drove five minutes in the other direction to that in which Alexis had gone.

She was stunned at how eager Craig was to get her out of the car when he drew into the parking lot and said, "Have fun! Work hard!" and drove off almost before she'd closed the door.

The vampire stood at the front door of the small building and stared at the AL'S SEAFOOD sign that hung from the edge of the roof.

A bell triggered when she pulled the old wooden door open, and it jingled cheerfully. The distinctive smell of fresh fish saturated the air, which was slightly jarring after the clear air outside. Her gaze moved automatically to the counter, but she didn't see anyone.

"Hello?" She took a few steps forward.

"One second. I'll be out in a minute," a voice called from the back of the store.

While she waited, she studied the small shop that held a surprisingly wide variety of foods. On her left, a long bank of freezers displayed everything from cakes to frozen fish to lobster tails. Several shelves of dry goods and seasonings stood in the center. As if to greet her when she walked in, a tank held live but sluggish lobsters.

Her exploration moved to the stacked cases. Directly ahead, Vickie noticed a fresh seafood case loaded with skinless, headless creatures from the sea packed in ice and surrounded by kale garnishes. One-third of the container held various sizes of shrimp, both cooked and raw.

On the right side, near the register, was a long case of deli salads—fruit salad, bean salad, tuna salad, crab salad… the list went on. Beside these were several cheesecakes, which excited her. *I wonder how many of these I can eat on the job.*

A menu hung above the display. *It looks like they serve fish buckets, burgers, fries...so much good food. How does a place this small do so doggone much?*

She would have her answer soon, as an old woman with obviously dyed blonde hair dragged her feet into the front area and greeted her with a smile. "Hey there. I'm Kathy. You must be Vickie. Come on around. When you come back next time, you can use the back entrance. You'll get a key."

Vickie walked behind the counter and followed the woman past a dishwashing room with a long row of sinks on one side and a cooking area with a grill, oven, and deep fryer on the other.

In the back, a countertop stretched along the wall. On top of that was a neatly folded beige shirt that bore the Al's Seafood logo of a fish wearing a chef's hat. "Go ahead and put that on, sweetie. Then go into the closet back there and grab yourself an apron." She complied and soon, she looked like a regular employee.

Kathy waved her over to an old copper-colored machine mounted on the wall with large white paper cards beside it. "This is how you punch in. Grab a new card, write your name on it, and slip it in here." When she slid the card into the slot, the machine made a loud clicking sound, and the woman showed her the date and time stamped on it.

"That's so cool." She punched in herself eagerly.

Her companion laughed. "If that impresses you, then you'll love this job. Let's go get your hands dirty. Follow me."

She led her to a large metal door with a huge handle on it and pulled it open to reveal a walk-in cooler with boxes of fish and cheesecakes stacked everywhere. "Go ahead and grab that box of cod there and take it to the room with the sinks in, okay?"

As Vickie hauled the carton to the designated area, Kathy followed with two big blue plastic bins off one of the shelves outside the cooler and another big box that was unmarked.

She grunted as she hoisted it all onto the countertop. "Okay, job number one—breading cod. Our top seller is fried cod and fried haddock. But we don't actually sell haddock. Both are actually cod and we tell them it's haddock. No one knows the difference anyway. Go ahead and open that box and pour the breadcrumbs into one of those bins.

The vampire ripped the box open and dumped the contents into a container, unleashing a cloud of dust into the air.

"Oh, yeah, I forgot to warn you about that. Okay, one bin is for breading and one bin is for storage. Take a piece of cod out of that box, drop it in there, and swish it around until it's coated, then drop it into the new bin."

"That's it?"

"That's it. It ain't rocket science, sweetie. Oh...do you have a hat at home?" She pointed to Vickie's head.

"Uh, no."

"Okay, that's fine for today but pull your hair back into a ponytail. Otherwise, you either have to cut it short like mine, wear a hairnet, or wear a hat. I'll let you choose, but with that beautiful hair, you'll probably want a hat. I'll be out sweeping and mopping the floors, so holler if you need something." Kathy walked away and left her alone with a giant box of fish.

She leaned forward and squinted through the window to make sure the other employee wasn't paying attention. At a rapid speed, she threw each piece of cod from the box, one by one, into the breadcrumbs.

That done, she paused again to make sure she didn't have an audience. Then, she tapped into her super-strength, shook the bin, and launched the fish and the breadcrumbs into the air. With a flick of her wrist, she managed to keep the coating moving in a circular pattern as if she were stir-frying in a wok.

After a few seconds of this, she slammed the bin down hard on the countertop. Kathy, who was still sweeping, looked up to see what the noise was. Vickie waved innocently, and the woman returned to her task.

The vampire worked quickly to remove each piece of cod at lightning speed and stacked them in the final bin. She finished the entire job in about two and a half minutes.

Her satisfaction was a little dampened by the realization that her superhuman speed would definitely look too suspicious and she had to wait for a while before she finally announced that she was done. She looked at the fresh seafood case during those moments of idleness. *So this is what it's like to have a job, huh?*

CHAPTER TWENTY-SEVEN

"You smell."

Alexis greeted Vickie with those words after she arrived home from her first shift at Al's Seafood.

"Hey, give me a break. I breaded fish for, like, three hours." She held her hands up. "I think my skin is more fish than vampire at this point."

Her sister laughed at her as she headed to her room to ready herself for a long, hot shower. As she unbuttoned her shirt, she smiled. *You have a nice job. It's not too difficult so far. You'll earn a little spending money, and you have a bank account you can fill up with podcast money. Life is good.*

But when she dropped her shirt into the basket, a folded piece of paper fell from the breast pocket. "Oh right." She bent to retrieve her schedule, which she had been given before she left after her shift but hadn't looked at yet.

Really? Her face twisted in confusion. She hadn't thought too much about when she would work. There weren't enough hours during the week to be able to do so after school, so most of her work hours were on the weekends—Friday night, Saturday, and Sunday.

She opened her bedroom door and walked out, still holding the schedule. "Can you believe this? I'm working, like, every weekend. When will I see Eric? Or hang out with friends?"

"Let me see." Alexis took it from her and studied it quickly. "It's not so bad. You'll be off by nine most of the time. And Sunday, you only work until four. You'll have to hang out late at night if everyone is still hanging. Because seriously, you'll need to shower before you go anywhere. Woof!" She pinched her nose and handed the schedule back to Vickie, who threw it into her room and headed to the bathroom.

While in the shower, she couldn't shake her frustration at this unexpected and unpleasant development. *I have a great boyfriend and now, I won't be able to see him. This sucks. I want a normal life. Did I really have to get this job?*

For a moment, she considered telling her boss she couldn't work the whole weekend, but then she remembered there was a minimum hours requirement, and the only way she could reach that minimum was to put in all those weekend hours.

After her shower, she changed into sweats and wandered into the living room and plopped down on the couch, her mood a little depressed.

Craig looked up from his chair. "What's the matter, working girl? Are you tired after a long day?"

The vampire sighed. "Yeah, but that's not why I'm bummed. I've settled into things with Eric and now, I have to spend all my free time at work."

"Oh, it's probably not so bad."

When she explained her schedule, he lapsed into thought for a moment. "Okay, that's not exactly good. But hey, that's the life of an employee. You have to get your hours in somewhere."

She twiddled her thumbs where she slouched on the couch. "Sure, and I won't be able to see my boyfriend."

He smiled. "Can I tell you a story?"

Vickie looked at him with skepticism. "If I say no, would you tell it anyway?"

"Probably. When Alexis's mom and I were dating, I took a job in customer service at a department store. It was an awful job, but I needed the money at the time. It was right around the start of this job that I asked her to marry me."

"Okay…where are you going with this?" She knew he had the tendency to go off at a tangent unless kept firmly on track.

"Stick with me here. The job was the second shift. Carol worked from nine to five during weekdays and had weekends off. I worked from one thirty in the afternoon until ten at night, and every other weekend."

She twisted her face in disgust. "That's a terrible schedule."

"Tell me about it. I took it thinking I could work my way into a first shift position, but any time one opened up, they gave it to someone else. It never failed. I worked there for the entire year we were engaged."

"You didn't go out on many dates then." She laughed.

"Rarely. We would hang out on my days off or see each other between shifts, or whatever. We couldn't simply go out on a Saturday night or anything because I had to work. It put a real strain on our relationship."

"That's brutal. What did you do?"

"I called her. Every single night. She was usually getting ready for bed by then, but I called her as soon as I left the office building and could turn my phone on. I walked across the parking lot in the pitch dark—I had to park far from the door because I arrived during the day when all the first shifters were there, and they had all the good spaces."

"This sounds like the worst job ever." She shook her head as she tried to imagine it.

"That's not my point. I called every night and walked to the car while I talked to her on the phone about her day. After about five or ten minutes, I'd be out of energy and she'd be ready for bed, so we'd say goodnight and hang up. I did this almost every night for a year."

"You'd just got engaged to this girl, and you barely saw her and only spent a few minutes on the phone with her at night? What a miserable life." She straightened. "Are you only trying to make me feel better about my current situation?"

"No, although you do get to see Eric in school, so your situation is technically better than mine. No, what I'm trying to say is, love finds a way. We did our best to at least connect every day, even if it was only for a few minutes. That's because it was important to us. And even though we didn't see each other as much as we would have liked to, we still kept the relationship going because we both wanted to."

"Do you think Eric and I will be able to keep our relationship going, even if we don't see each other that much?"

Craig gave her a sympathetic smile. "I don't know. Only you two can answer that. But what I will say is that it probably won't be as hard as you think. You'll merely be very busy. And that's okay. At least you'll get a little money in exchange."

Vickie smiled. "Thanks. You know, I don't think you've talked about your engagement before. How did you do it?"

"Propose? Well, you know how I said we got engaged right around the time I started that job?" She nodded. "We actually got engaged on the very first day."

"Yeah?" She leaned forward and rested her elbows on her knees.

"Yep. I had steady work for the first time in a long time, and I knew I wanted to propose to her. I didn't know how to buy an engagement ring, so after I finished work on my first day, I went to a jeweler at Mayfair Mall. I chose the ring that I liked, and I asked about financing options. He said, 'Oh, you can get that one for no money down once you're approved, and the payments begin next month. Suddenly, my hands started to shake."

"Why?" She smirked, entertained by the thought of him being that nervous.

"Because I knew that once I could get my hands on a ring, I would propose almost immediately. When he said no money down, it meant I could leave with the ring that day. I pulled my phone out and left a message with Carol, asking her to meet me at my apartment when she finished work because I had something for her."

The vampire raised a finger. "Wait a second. I thought you were working second shift."

He shook his head. "The first week was training, and that meant you worked first shift but only for that week."

"A tease." She laughed.

"You're not kidding! And speaking of tease, I stopped at my parents' house to let them know I planned to propose that night. I also wanted to pick up some candles so I could be all romantic about it and I knew my mom would have some. While we were discussing it, I received texts from Carol asking if we're breaking up."

She burst out laughing. "No kidding?"

"Oh yeah! See, she kept asking questions and I kept telling her, 'Just talk to me tonight.' All that vagueness really bothered her. She was a classic overthinker. I took the candles and the ring, ran home, changed into one of her favorite outfits of mine, lit the candles, and put them all over my apartment. She walked in and poked her head around the corner, scared to death."

"And then you proposed." She smiled warmly.

"You got it. Little did she know that she would spend the next year engaged to a guy she would barely see. I don't miss those days. But they did make us stronger as a couple."

Vickie sighed and imagined getting engaged. *Back home, I would be married by now. Although it would probably be much less romantic.* "I hope Eric and I can make it through this."

Craig stood and folded his arms. "Put it this way—if you don't, you two weren't meant to be. But if you are, you'll be just fine. Take advantage of the time you have and power through the time you don't. You'll do great."

"Thanks." Vickie stretched out on the couch as he walked out of the room.

Alexis wandered in and sat at her feet. "If you're going to smell like that at the end of every shift, Eric is the one who will be thankful for the time apart." She gave her a teasing smile.

The vampire kicked her playfully. "At least I don't have creepy dudes staring at me while I'm trying to work."

Her sister rolled her eyes. "That guy is so bad. Ugh! He makes me want to quit, but I kinda like the job. I didn't think I would."

"Mmm. Me too." Vickie tucked her hands behind her head. "I hate the hours, but the job is actually easy, and I have access to tons of good food."

"I tell you what," the other girl said as she looked out the window, "I didn't expect us to find jobs this quickly. Growing up sure happens fast."

"Don't remind me. One day, you go to bed and the next day, it's four hundred years later."

Alexis cocked an eyebrow. "That's not what I meant."

CHAPTER TWENTY-EIGHT

Once she'd showered after another shift at Al's Seafood and holed up in her room, Vickie messaged Eric on her computer. It was a Saturday night, and he had gone out with their friends.

Eric: *I really wish you didn't have to work*

Vickie: *I know, but it's a new job. My uncle says I have to start making money*

Vickie: *I feel really bad about it*

Eric: *I'm not trying to make you feel bad, I'm sorry - just missed you tonight, that's all*

After a few minutes of this, she logged off for the evening and looked forward to a good night of sleep after six hours of being on her feet.

Unfortunately, rest wasn't on the cards.

As soon as she began to drift off, her stomach twisted again. *No. Not now. Please. It's late. I'm exhausted. I want to sleep.*

But her sense of danger refused to let her relax. She was about to wake Craig to warn him to get his gun again when she stepped out of her bedroom and looked out the bay window overlooking the field.

Three torches shined in the distance in the middle of the field. *How does anyone not see this?*

In her agitated state, she failed to realize that most of the houses that overlooked that particular field were owned by older couples who were all asleep at two in the morning.

She deliberated in the hallway. *Wake him up and put him at risk again? Chase them away and then what? They come back again? This needs to end.*

The vampire walked into the kitchen and selected a large chef's knife from the magnetic knife rack. *Attack them hard and go in swinging.* Although she was confident in her abilities, she wasn't sure if she would be able to defeat them if they had the sword.

She slipped her shoes on and turned to face the interior of the house one more time. *I really hope this isn't the last time I walk out of this house.* Undeterred, however, she opened the side door and slipped out.

The snow crunched under her shoes as she reached the top of the hill overlooking the basin of the field where the three shadowy figures stood. She twirled the knife in her hand and grasped it tightly. *Aim for the main guy. Make your first strike really count, because you'll only have one chance.*

Resolute, she took a deep breath, surged forward, and raced toward Gabriel as fast as she could, the knife held out in front of her. When she came within the last ten feet of them, however, her speed suddenly faltered.

Vickie almost fell face-first into the dirt but was able to

stay upright enough to ride the momentum to her target and drive the blade deep into his stomach.

The man grunted and fell, and his blood spilled onto the snow. Gasping for air, Vickie crawled away from them as his two companions rushed to tend to their leader.

Through gritted teeth, he still barked instructions. "The sword works. She has no power. Take her."

The two spun toward her, but although she appeared to have lost her powers, she still retained the agility and speed of a teenage athlete. She darted and dodged to evade them as much as she could.

When she came too close to Gabriel, he managed to grasp her pant leg. Vickie struggled to free herself and he laughed. Instead, she clutched the handle of the knife and yanked it violently out of his midsection. Waves of pain radiated throughout his body and forced him to release her.

She slashed the knife viciously and caught one of the other men on the side of the face. Quickly, she realized that the third—the man she had not touched yet—was Hannes, who had taken shot from Craig the last time they surrounded the house.

The vampire kept them at bay with the knife, which dripped and splattered blood as she swung it. "Why are we out here? What made you do this out here instead?"

The leader coughed and wheezed while he tried to maintain his composure despite the immense pain. "You were too protected in that house. You had others on your side. Out here, you could come alone."

"What will it be then, boys? Huh? If you want me dead,

you'll have to kill me fast because otherwise, I'll take you with me."

"Hannes, grab the sword." Gabriel raised his head weakly. "Fulfill the prophecy. Rid the world of the vampire race once and for all."

Vickie smiled. "You guys don't know about the other one, then?"

Hannes paused. "What other one?"

"The other vampire. There's a Sanguinarian over here, too. I don't know where he is right now, but I've fought with him for weeks. You can kill me, but you'll leave another one alive. And then what? You've accomplished nothing."

The assassins paused to think things over, which Vickie used an opportunity to lunge at them with the knife. This time, she sliced Hannes' arm and he dropped the sword and moaned in pain.

Vickie stooped to pick the weapon up, but a boot thumped into the side of her head. Jannik towered over her and shoved his boot to her chest while her ears rang from the blow.

Gabriel rolled weakly to his side to watch it unfold. He smiled as the blood dripped from his mouth. "Yes. Jannik, it is time. Fulfill the prophecy. Cement the legacy of the Slayer Circle. Let me watch the final extermination of the vampire race with my dying breath."

The assassin raised the sword over his head, ready to sever her head. Vickie pressed it into the snow, tightened her neck, and prepared for her death.

To her surprise, a rapid blur materialized seemingly from nowhere and flung the man away from her. The would-be killer uttered a guttural cry of horror as he fell heavily.

What the– Will stood over Jannik, a big, bloody smile on his face as he slid his fangs from his victim's neck.

"Will! Seriously?" She couldn't believe her eyes.

In the bright moonlight, his eyes seemed to glow with rage as he walked up to a frozen Hannes, who had no idea how to react. Thanks to the sword, the Sang had no speed anymore, but he didn't need it.

The man had given up out of fear. Will simply sauntered up to him and latched on to drain the blood from his body.

Vickie scowled in disgust, even though she was happy to see him. Once he had done enough damage to them, he turned to Gabriel who was already dying.

He pressed his boot into the leader's stomach and put his weight on it, forcing him to scream in pain. Will leaned forward and looked deep into his eyes as he whispered, "You will never rid the world of us. We will always come back—and when we do, your blood is ours."

The Sang lifted the sword, plunged it deep into Gabriel's belly, and pinned him to the ground as he took his last breaths. His body twitched and finally went still.

The vampire, however, would not get up. She watched his actions closely, suspicious of his intent, but he turned to her and extended his hand to help her to her feet. "Are you all right?"

She dusted the snow from her clothes. "I'm a little banged up, but I'm fine. Where did you come from?"

"I have been checking on you every night for weeks now. Only from a distance. When I saw the Circle guys assemble in the field, I watched from the other side of the hill over there. I wanted to see what they would do."

"You saved my life."

Will shrugged. "You made some good points the last time we spoke. Either way, I have to hide. There's no sense in trying to rid the world of humans if it's only me doing all the work. But I have to say, ridding the world of guys like these is something I'd be happy to do."

She looked at them with disgust. "We need to, like, bury that sword. I don't ever want to see it again."

"I'll do it. I'll take care of the bodies, too." She didn't ask any questions. "Go get cleaned up and get some sleep."

"What, we're friends now? We've tried to kill each other a few times, and that's it?" Vickie folded her arms. "You've put me and my family through a heck of a lot."

Will shook his head, chuckled, and wiped the blood from his chin. "I wouldn't say friends. Let's simply say we are free to coexist now."

"I can handle that. Where will you go? Will you come back to school?" She really was tired of hearing people ask about him.

"I'm not a human, Vickie. And unlike you, I don't want to be. I'm fine staying under the radar for now. I don't know where I'll go, but it won't be back to high school."

Reluctantly, Vickie gave him a hug. "Thanks for the help with these guys. My family tried to help, but they couldn't quite finish the job."

"Of course not. You needed another vampire." He smiled.

"You are not a vampire. You're still a sick freak. Don't ever tell me what you do with those bodies." She shook her head and walked back to the house, gradually feeling stronger and more filled with her vampire power with each step farther from the sword.

When she walked in the door, she caught Alexis staring out the bay window. "What happened out there?" she whispered.

"Let's say the problem is solved and leave it at that. We don't have to worry about the Circle anymore." Without elaborating, she went straight to bed and fell into a deep sleep.

CHAPTER TWENTY-NINE

The next morning, Vickie explained to Craig and Alexis what happened out in the field.

He immediately walked over to the bay window and squinted to try to see into the distance. "I don't see anything out there—no blood, nothing. I do see a clearing where I assume the activity took place, but other than that, there's nothing."

She was not surprised. "Will made it very clear that he would take care of everything and there would be no evidence left. Take that to mean whatever you want."

The other girl stared at the top of the kitchen table. "So Will actually saved you?"

"I'm as surprised as you are." She still had a hard time believing it. "But he was there. He attacked with a vengeance and brought the Circle's plans to a very decisive end. It was brutal."

"I still won't sit here and celebrate it." Alexis shifted in her chair. "I mean, that's still the guy who tried to kill me. He's still the guy who tried to kill you too."

"No one has to celebrate Will, okay?" Craig returned to his seat at the table. "He's a feral animal, trying to survive in the only way he knows. That's fine. But that's why I have a gun—to protect my family from feral animals. This time, he did some good. But if he comes here looking for you—"

"I don't think that'll be a problem," the vampire interjected quickly. "He told me he would go into hiding. I don't know where he'll go, but I doubt very much that he'll show up in biology class or something on Monday. He's gone."

Craig took her hand. "Search your head. Listen to your gut. Do you feel safe? Do you feel like you're no longer under any threat?"

Vickie wore a relaxed smile. "For the first time in months, honestly, yes. I really, really do. I feel great. No more Circle. No more Will. I am free to simply exist. Now, I can be Vickie Hewitt and not have to fight for my life anymore. I'm still tired from last night, of course, but in a day or two, I'll feel really good."

"I, for one, am excited to get back to a normal life," he announced as he walked to the stovetop and turned on the light on the hood. "I'll make my famous pancakes this morning to celebrate."

The girls were happy. They could now move forward knowing they were safe, and they could return to their original problems of keeping Vickie's powers under wraps and adjusting her to the modern human world.

As they sat at the table with a stack of pancakes on each plate, Craig raised his glass of orange juice. "To the new normal."

Later in the morning, the three of them piled into the SUV and dropped Alexis off at the Bradley Road Market.

Vickie gave her a high-five as she moved to the front seat of the SUV.

This feels so weird. I know this is basically how it was when I first came here, but it feels so fresh and new. And free!

She climbed into the front seat and shut the door.

"I have a surprise for you." Craig smiled at her while she fastened her seatbelt. "You'll see."

They pulled into the parking lot of the electronics store. "What are we doing here?"

"Come on." He slid out, led her smugly into the store, and walked to the displays of cell phones.

The vampire grew cautiously excited. "Does this mean what I think it means?"

"Now, look—there will be some hard rules about this. But one of the reasons we had such problems last time you were out with Eric was because we didn't have an open line of communication. I have one with Alexis, and that's not fair to you. I told myself I wouldn't let you simply have a phone for fun but only if there was a practical need for one. Now, there is."

Vickie almost jumped with excitement. She threw her arms around him and squeezed tightly. "Thank you!"

"You're welcome. But listen, you have money now, and a bank account. I don't want you to empty it. I'll give you a hundred and fifty dollars toward any unlocked phone you want. Then, when we get home, I can add it to our family plan."

While she pored over the phones, he stood aside and watched her. *She barely knows how to handle herself out there. She's getting better, but still... I hope this isn't a huge mistake, letting her have access to a phone. She's a teenager. She's in high school. They all have phones. I simply have to teach her how to be responsible about it. What did Carol say to me all the time when I complained about stuff like this?*

"It's called parenting, Craig." You're right, my love.

Brimming with excitement, she chose her phone and they brought it home. While Craig was on his laptop to add it to their family plan and activate it, he gave her a stern warning.

"Do whatever you want on here. But if I think you're misusing it, I have full access to this phone's minutes, texts, and data from my laptop and my phone. I can switch it off any time I want. There have to be boundaries, and you can't misuse this."

"Of course. Thank you so much." She cradled the phone in her hands like a baby and laughed with joy.

"It's all set up now, so you should be good to go. Carry it with you whenever you leave this house, you hear me?"

"Of course. I won't go anywhere without it." She immediately opened the Facebook app and messaged Eric to ask for his cell number. Minutes later, she had him on the phone and was chatting up a storm. She disappeared quickly into her bedroom for privacy.

"It's called parenting, Craig. You can't avoid it." He sighed to himself as he closed his laptop.

CHAPTER THIRTY

"Hey, Jim, can I talk to you for a second?"

Jim Trembo looked up from his desk. He leaned back in his office chair, ran his fingers through his auburn hair, and straightened his glasses. "Do you have something for me, Pete?"

The man stepped in and closed the office door. He carried an open laptop. A small, nebbish little man, Pete Stabone was part of a special operations team that Jim oversaw.

He sat in the chair opposite his supervisor and stared silently at his screen.

"Pete? Do you plan to talk, or can I get back to work here?"

"Oh! Sorry. We have one of our first big hits from Operation Superball."

Jim nodded with delight. Operation Superball was a quiet government initiative designed to conduct a deep scan of the United States for supernatural activity by measuring the electromagnetic fields for odd spikes in activity.

It was a project near and dear to Trembo's heart, as he had a love for the supernatural and long suspected that more was happening than met the eye.

He clapped briskly when he heard the news from Pete. "I cashed in many favors to get this project off the ground. Literally. I knew it would produce something eventually."

A series of electromagnetic field sensors were floated above the country under the guise of weather balloons. No one would suspect a thing, and they could conduct these measurements without anyone knowing what they were doing.

"Now, Pete, before you get me all excited, we've floated these sensors all over the place for months. The occasional spike here and there doesn't mean anything. We have to make sure that these are, almost literally, off-the-charts readings. That's the only way you'll get me to jump on board. What do you have?"

"Ah...well, Boss, we have quite the reading here." He tapped his keyboard a few times to pull up the right record. "It's over Milwaukee, Wisconsin, actually."

"Milwaukee? That's a smallish city by comparison to others, even though it's the largest in Wisconsin. I can't say I'm too surprised. Smaller areas tend to have more of these things. What were the readings like, though?" He leaned forward to see for himself.

Pete propped up his laptop on the desk and spun it around. "It broke the stinking sensors, Jim. Fried them, actually."

His jaw dropped. He covered his mouth and leaned

back in his chair as he stifled a smile. "That's almost certainly proof of supernatural activity. My goodness. We have to investigate. Where exactly in Milwaukee was this located? Someone's house? A place of business? A church?"

The other man reclaimed his laptop and typed again to zoom in on the map. "No, no. It looks like it was in an open field. A flood reservoir, actually. Merely a big basin in an empty field."

"Hmm." His supervisor shook his head. "That isn't quite what I expected. I assumed a church would probably be the location. Okay, well, we can't argue with these results. Let's get to Milwaukee as soon as we can and see what we can find."

Pete leaned in with a smile. "Two years of research and testing and we finally have our first big result. How do you feel right now?"

He stood and looked out his window at the cherry trees. "I'm nervous, Pete, to be honest. I worry that this is some kind of false positive."

The investigator shook his head in disbelief. "Oh. come on—it broke the sensor. This can't be a false positive. If anything, it's a guarantee that something's going on in that field. Even the remnants of supernatural activity would trip the sensors strongly enough. A reading this crazy means there's probably still something there."

Jim faced the other man and smiled. "I hope there is. If so, then the fun has only started."

Twenty-four hours later, Jim, Pete, and a team of supernatural scientists wore various sensors and other equipment to determine the exact location of the readings. They trudged through the snow in the field until they reached a section of the clearing that had definitely seen supernatural activity.

All their sensors overloaded, and gauges snapped. A chill ran up Jim's spine. "This is crazy. I've never seen everything go haywire like this. And look at the indentations in this snow. It's definitely the site of something. There was activity, for sure."

Pete crouched in the snow, his nose barely inches from the ground. "Jim, can you send someone here to take samples? I think we have blood here."

He nodded to one of the scientists on staff who carefully approached the area in question. The technician scooped up a sample of the discolored snow and slipped it into a vial for analysis.

"Take a few more samples, guys." He pointed to a few different places. "Try to get as clear of a picture as possible of what might have happened here. We've obviously stumbled on some kind of presence."

"Hey guys, over here!" Another of the men waved them over to a place where recently turned dirt was visible on the surface of the ground under a light dusting of snow. "This is freshly dug. There's gotta be something under here."

The team leader looked excitedly at Pete. "You said there was probably something still here, didn't you?" He slapped him on the back and hurried over to the disturbance.

"It could be a dead body or a body part from a supernatural beast. Whatever it is, we'll take it with us." Jim muttered constantly to himself and his breath quickened as he dug quickly.

After a few minutes of scraping the dirt away with their hands, his fingers touched metal. He caught hold of it and dragged it out. For a few moments, those gathered simply stared at the strange antique sword they'd unearthed.

"I've never seen these designs in my life. This has to be related to whatever went on here. Who buried a sword in the middle of a field?"

"Don't get discouraged." Pete stepped beside him to inspect the sword himself. "This is absolutely a result. The sensors we launched picked up on this thing. Now, we simply have to determine where it came from."

Jim stood and turned his attention to the row of houses overlooking the field. His subordinate stepped beside him. "What are you thinking?"

"That someone in one of those houses probably knows about what went on out here. I can't imagine something this significant happened and no one saw it. We'll have to go door to door and maybe dig into the histories. I want to know who lives in these houses and where they came from."

The other man made a note on his phone and slipped it into his pocket. "You got it, boss. I'll get the orders in as soon as we reach the hotel."

He nodded, then turned to watch his team inspect the area closely. A brisk wind blew, and he shivered and shoved his hands in his pockets to hold his overcoat closed.

Some kind of beast—or something—was here. Maybe it was killed, and whoever did the deed buried the murder weapon. There are so many tests to run, I don't know where to start. But one thing is for sure. We'll spend some quality time here in Milwaukee for a while.

The End

The adventures and challenges don't end here. Why is the government agency interested in Vicki? Can Vicki and Alexis get past a disagreement and get along? The adventures continue with Vicki, Alexis and Craig in *THE GIRL UNLEASHED.*

FREE BOOKS!

WARNING:

The Troll is now in charge.

And he's giving away free books if you sign-up!

Join the only newsletter hosted by a Troll!

Get sneak peeks, exclusive giveaways, behind the scenes content, and more.
PLUS you'll be notified of special **one day only fan pricing** on new releases.

CLICK HERE

or visit: https://marthacarr.com/read-free-stories/

DARK IS HER NATURE

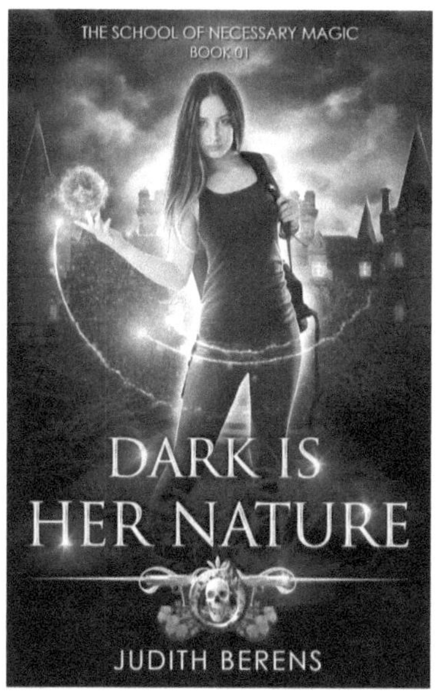

For Hire: Teachers for special school in Virginia countryside.

Must be able to handle teenagers with special abilities.

Cannot be afraid to discipline werewolves, wizards, elves and other assorted hormonal teens.

Apply at the School of Necessary Magic.

AVAILABLE AT AMAZON RETAILERS

THE PEABRAIN'S IDEA

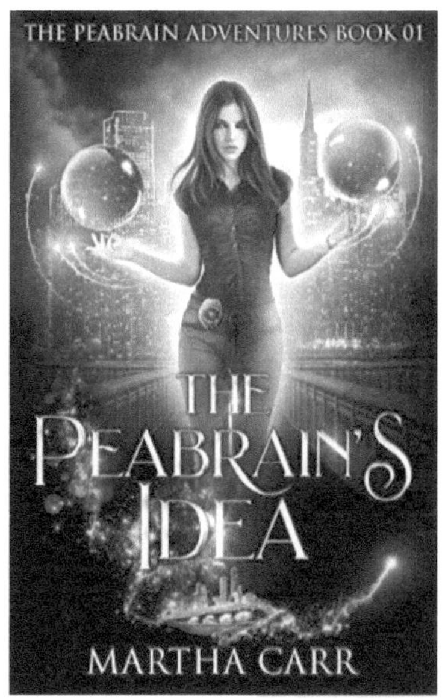

Find the compass, save the world or save herself?

Dating is harder for Maggie Parker than running down a felon. Now add in magic.

Did she just see a compass fly?

Can she learn how to use the magic of bubbles to chart a new course in time? It's a lot harder than it sounds.

Join her on her quest to rescue passengers on an ancient ship – a big blue marble called Earth – and save herself.

AUTHOR NOTES - MARTHA CARR

JULY 10, 2019

I'm about to turn 60 on September 6th and I see it as the last great (hopefully super long) chapter of my life. I'm looking to start this chapter with a few good changes. One of them is making peace with food and getting into better shape. It's a Peabrain Society goal for me. (More on that later)

I was a runner about twenty years ago. I loved it, especially after the first mile was behind me and my body got into the rhythm of the run. Breathing became easier, my legs relaxed, and it was a form of meditation.

Turns out twenty years might as well be a millennium. Recently, I kept running into a friend after she had gone on a run and she had that sweaty glow clinging to her. Her excitement at getting out on the road was contagious. I wanted some of that too.

Okay, so where to begin after so many years. A quick check of Runners World's site and I found an eight-week beginner's plan that seemed pretty simple. Week one - run a minute, walk two minutes, repeat ten times. Easy peasey. Turns out, you can bend time. A minute when running in even early morning Texas heat after so many years of sitting in a chair and staring at a computer feels a lot like five minutes. To my credit, I kept going on one of the sprints even though I had forgotten to set the timer, so maybe that one was two minutes…

Also, note to self – I count super fast. I can get to one hundred and eighty before my iPhone is willing to agree with me that a minute has gone by.

But, despite all of it, I kept going. I'm still going on Day 3. Already, I remember what it was like to see so much of my neighborhood from ground level and at a slower pace. I got to run by the new gym and a resort-style pool that opens in my neighborhood next week. I saw the old El Camino parked outside my neighbor's house that I used as inspiration in a new series.

Even better, when I got to the really steep hill and it was time to run… I ran. In the back of my mind I'm wondering if I'll have to do week one over again, which will be okay. It's the getting out there that matters. But, I'm also willing to just try it their way and flip the amount of running and walking and steadily increase the time.

Mostly, it's because I'm showing myself all over again that it's possible to set new goals, to change and to stretch, even when it's hard and victory seems kind of iffy. It's the journey that matters after all, far more than the destination. Hoping for a 5k in the winter and I plan to write on a white t-shirt, 'This is What 60 Looks Like' as I cruise past everyone. I'll let you know how it goes. By the way, The

Peabrain Society is something new I'm starting in my fan Facebook group to help us all go after our dreams – as a group. Come join us. More adventures to follow.

AUTHOR NOTES - MICHAEL ANDERLE

JULY 16, 2019

THANK YOU for not only reading this story but these *Author Notes* as well.

(I think I've been good with always opening with "thank you." If not, I need to edit the other *Author Notes*!)

RANDOM (*sometimes*) THOUGHTS?

Have you ever thought about buying a truck from an elf in Ohio, or a bag of groceries from a vampire on the night shift at a 7Eleven?

Normally, I don't.

However, there is an interesting paragraph with the truck comment in an upcoming book. Here it is:

It was a few minutes of walking through the woods until he made it to the road. It was almost completely empty except for an old early 2000s pickup truck. Most of the red tint had faded, but it still worked just as well as when he had first bought it off the elf in Ohio.

I just thought to myself, *Self, how different would it be if we* did *have normal everyday transactions with fantasy characters in real life?*

(Editor's note: How do you know we don't? I mean, have you been *in a Circle K at midnight? Whew! Could be any of those people)*

Which, of course, took me to a vampire at a 7-Eleven (at night of course.) How many random acts of violence would happen at *that* convenience store?

It's kind of like Kevin Smith's Clerks…for the paranormal world.

Now I need to go write this down.

AROUND THE WORLD IN 80 DAYS

One of the interesting (at least to me) aspects of my life is the ability to work from anywhere and at any time. In the future, I hope to re-read my own *Author Notes* and remember my life as a diary entry.

Cave in the Sky(TM) Las Vegas, Nevada

It's about 7:40PM (twelve hours after writing my previous set of *Author Notes*), and I'm ready to end my day.

This timing reminds me of a joke about a group of working people that went like this. "I only make them work half a day. I don't care if it is the first half or the second half, but it's only half a day."

I've finished my half a day, and the boss is pushing me to finish yet another project.

I think I'm going to sneak out of my office.

I hope your summer of 2019 is going fantastic! May you have time to read another twenty books before school kicks in for those who attend, or who have kids who attend.

If life has you down, read another book.

FAN PRICING

$0.99 Saturdays (new LMBPN stuff) and $0.99 Wednesday (both LMBPN books and friends of LMBPN books.) Get great stuff from us and others at tantalizing prices.

Go ahead. I bet you can't read just one.

Sign up here: http://lmbpn.com/email/.

HOW TO MARKET FOR BOOKS YOU LOVE

Review them so others have your thoughts, and tell friends and the dogs of your enemies (because who wants to talk to enemies?)... *Enough said ;-)*

Ad Aeternitatem,

Michael Anderle

SERIES IN THE ORICERAN UNIVERSE:

JOIN THE ORICERAN UNIVERSE FAN GROUP ON FACEBOOK!

BOOKS BY MICHAEL ANDERLE

For a complete list of books by Michael Anderle, please visit

www.lmbpn.com/ma-books/

All LMBPN Audiobooks are Available at Audible.com and iTunes. For a complete list of audiobooks visit:

www.lmbpn.com/audible

CONNECT WITH THE AUTHORS

Martha Carr Social

Website: http://www.marthacarr.com

Facebook: https://www.facebook.com/groups/MarthaCarrFans/

Michael Anderle Social

Michael Anderle Social
Website:
http://www.lmbpn.com

Email List:
http://lmbpn.com/email/

Facebook Here: https://www.facebook.com/TheKurtherianGambitBooks/

www.ingramcontent.com/pod-product-compliance
Lightning Source LLC
Chambersburg PA
CBHW050247110726
47898CB00007B/2316

* 9 7 8 1 6 4 2 0 2 3 7 4 9 *